R

"*I'm pregnant,*"

Joanie told J.D. as she got out of the car. "I don't expect anything from you. I just felt you should know."

She waited as he sat behind the wheel, staring out the windshield, a blank look on his face.

She understood his shock, felt terrible that she was the cause of it, but was convinced she'd done the right thing in telling him about her pregnancy. He had a right to know he'd fathered a child.

She wished that there had been a better way to break the news, a gentler method of making him aware, but in the end, the simplest words were the only ones she could form. "*I'm pregnant.*" Innocent in their simplicity, but damning in delivery.

Dear Reader,

Happy Valentine's Day! Love is in the air, and Special Edition has plenty of little cupids to help matchmake! There are family stories here, there are breathtaking romances there—you name it, you'll find love in each and every Silhouette Special Edition.

This month we're pleased to welcome new-to-Silhouette author Angela Benson. Her debut book for Special Edition, *A Family Wedding*, is a warm, wonderful tale of friends falling in love...and a darling little girl's dream come true.

We're also proud to present Jane Toombs's dramatic tale, *Nobody's Baby*, our THAT'S MY BABY! title. Jane also has written under the pseudonym Diana Stuart, and this is her first book for Special Edition under her real name. And speaking of firsts, please welcome to Special Edition, veteran Silhouette Desire author Peggy Moreland, by reading *Rugrats and Rawhide*—a tender tale of love for this Valentine's month.

Sherryl Woods returns with a marvelous new series— THE BRIDAL PATH. Don't miss the first book, *A Ranch for Sara*, a rollicking, heartwarming love story. The second and third titles will be available in March and April! And the Valentine's Day thermostat continues to rise with Gina Wilkins's sparkling tale of opposites attracting in *The Father Next Door*.

Finally, Natalie Bishop presents readers with the perfect February title—*Valentine's Child*. This tale of love lost and then rediscovered is full of the Valentine's Day spirit!

I hope you enjoy this book, and each and every title to come!

Sincerely,

Tara Gavin, Senior Editor

Please address questions and book requests to:
Silhouette Reader Service
U.S.: 3010 Walden Ave., P.O. Box 1325, Buffalo, NY 14269
Canadian: P.O. Box 609, Fort Erie, Ont. L2A 5X3

PEGGY MORELAND
RUGRATS AND RAWHIDE

Published by Silhouette Books
America's Publisher of Contemporary Romance

To my nieces and nephews...Cara, Clint and
Cassie Crews; Natalie, Brett and Lorri Morse;
Kendall and Michael O'Neal; Clint and Julie Hibbard.

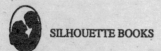 SILHOUETTE BOOKS

ISBN 0-373-24084-8

RUGRATS AND RAWHIDE

Copyright © 1997 by Peggy Bozeman Morse

Printed in U.S.A.

Books by Peggy Moreland

Silhouette Special Edition

Rugrats and Rawhide #1084

Silhouette Desire

A Little Bit Country #515
Run for the Roses #598
Miss Prim #682
The Rescuer #765
Seven Year Itch #837
The Baby Doctor #867
Miss Lizzy's Legacy #921
A Willful Marriage #1024

PEGGY MORELAND

published her first romance novel with Silhouette in 1989. She's a natural storyteller with a sense of humor that will tickle your fancy, and Peggy's goal is to write a story that readers will remember long after the last page is turned. Winner of the 1992 National Reader's Choice Award and a 1994 RITA finalist, Peggy frequently appears on bestseller lists around the country. A native Texan, she and her family live in Round Rock, Texas.

J. D. CAWTHON AND JOANIE SUMMERS'S RULES FOR COHABITATION

(FOR A PERIOD OF SIX MONTHS)

Rule #1: No prancing around in anything that even remotely resembles lingerie or boxer shorts. Shirts are required at all times.

Rule #2: The bathroom is reserved for bouts of morning sickness from 6:00 a.m. until 10:00 a.m. All other times, it's whoever gets there first.

Rule #3: Joanie is required to prepare a meal for J.D. consisting of something other than pizza or hot dogs at least one night a week.

Rule #4: All children must reserve their horseback riding to broomsticks or overturned barrels and refrain from attempting to ride J.D.'s thoroughbred stock.

Rule #5: The word *marriage* will not be mentioned at any time, by either party, for any purpose. Doing so nullifies all prior agreements.

Chapter One

"Oh, my stars! Would you get a load of what just walked in the door."

Sitting at a table at San Antonio's favorite country and western dance hall, the Watering Hole, Joanie didn't hear her friend Serena's comment. It wasn't the loud music that kept her from hearing, although it was deafening. It was something far more remote. Her thoughts were centered over a hundred miles away and on her children who were spending the weekend with their grandparents. It took a sound kick in the shin to grab her attention away from her worries.

"What?" she asked, turning to frown at Serena.

Serena nodded toward the entrance. "Get a load of what just walked in."

Since she'd heard this same comment at least a dozen times over the past couple of hours and was

beginning to develop a neck ache from twisting around
to look at the men Serena spotted, Joanie didn't bother
to respond to her friend's request. Granted, the men
Serena had pointed out were all handsome enough, but
Joanie's heart simply wasn't in scoping out the male
population. She was too busy worrying about her children. This was the first time they'd spent an entire
weekend away from her, and although Joanie knew
her ex-in-laws would take care of the twins, Joanie
couldn't help but worry.

"Joanie!" Serena insisted.

Heaving a sigh, Joanie dutifully turned to follow the
line of her friend's gaze to the entrance. But at the
sight of the man standing there, she sucked the breath
right back in. Her heart took a plunging dive to her
stomach and bounced back up to lodge in her throat.

"J. D. Cawthon," she murmured, her eyes round in
disbelief.

"Who?" Serena asked, straining to get a better
glimpse.

"J. D. Cawthon," Joanie repeated.

"Do you know him?"

Joanie stared, memories flipping like pictures in an
album over a span of fifteen years. Years of standing
on the sidelines watching him, almost bodily throwing
herself at him at every opportunity, but always too
young and too much the kid sister to be taken seri-
ously. Years of watching him ride broncs at the rodeos, her heart in her throat, her hands squeezed tight
between her knees while she made all sorts of deals
with God to keep J.D. safe for her. She wondered if
J.D. realized it had been her prayers that had saved

him many a time from the flying hooves of a wild bronc.

"Sort of," she replied absently, still unable to believe she was seeing him again after so many years. "He was a friend of my brother George. They used to ride the rodeo circuit together."

Serena propped her elbow on the table and her hand on her cheek. "Wow," she murmured with a lustful sigh as she and Joanie both watched J.D. shoulder his way through the crowd.

At the edge of the dance floor he stopped, cocking his hands at his hips while he scanned the crowd, his eyes narrowed against the thick layer of smoke that hung over the room like a cloud. He looked almost the same as Joanie remembered him. Granted, he'd aged a bit, but he still carried that same air of arrogant maleness that had made her drool as a teenager and even now had the power to make her heart kick into a faster gear.

Shirtsleeves cuffed to his elbows revealed muscled arms and a smattering of soft, dark hair the same shade as that which peeked from beneath the cowboy hat shadowing his face. His hair was cut conservatively at the ears just as it had been ten years ago when she'd last seen him, but now he wore the back longer, letting it brush his collar.

He was tall, about six foot three, and built like a whiplash, his body fluid but honed with the muscular strength required of a bronc rider. A cavalry-style shirt stretched across the breadth of his chest, the brass buttons forming an inverted triangle from shoulder to navel that seemed to point like an arrow at something just below his belt. Like a fool, Joanie let her gaze drop, following the point of the arrow to the spot of denim faded a lighter shade that covered the subtle bulge at his fly...and wondered as she had as a teenager what lay sleeping behind that thin wall of denim.

She glanced away, her cheeks flaming, stricken by her own carnal thoughts. Her gaze met Serena's and she groaned, knowing by her friend's grin that Serena had read her mind.

"All right, so maybe I am as sexually deprived as you seem to think I am," she admitted grudgingly.

Laughing, Serena reached over to pat Joanie's hand. "You are. That's why I brought you here."

Though she tried her darnedest not to, Joanie couldn't resist stealing another look J.D.'s way. He remained at the edge of the dance floor, watching the dancers through narrowed eyes. He was easy enough to identify. A wide silver buckle held a tooled leather belt at his waist. Carved on the back of the worn leather strip were the initials, *J.D.* Cautiously, Joanie let her gaze drift lower, skipping from belt buckle to thigh, not daring to let her eyes linger at his fly. Then, more slowly, she trailed the almost-white line that creased the length of his starched denim jeans to boots polished just short of a shine.

Unlike most of the men in the room who'd dressed for the evening to create an image, Joanie knew J.D.'s wardrobe was genuine. From the crown of his hand-creased Stetson to the run-down heels of his boots, he was a cowboy through and through. Unable to believe that she was actually seeing him again after so many years, Joanie let her gaze shift back to his face. There was nothing pretty about the face shadowed by the Stetson hat. J.D.'s features were rugged, carved by the

odd mixture of ancestors who'd sired him. Nature had
had a hand in his coloring, though—eyes the deep,
clear blue of a cloudless Texas sky; skin stained by
an unrelenting sun to the same unique shade of umber
as the Central Texas soil; hair as black as Satan's
heart. A few broncs had left their marks on his face,
as well. A scar cut through his left brow; another ran
the length of one cheek. He wore both with the pride
of medals won in battle.

No, by no stretch of the imagination was J.D. a
handsome man, not in the sense most women judged,
but Joanie found him as appealing as she had at the
age of thirteen.

There was something about him, a wildness coupled
with a commanding air backed by muscled strength
that made every woman who met him dream of taming
him…and made every man who met him cut a wide
girth.

It had been years since Joanie had been around
horses, but seeing J.D. standing there at the edge of
the dance floor reminded her of a proud stallion watching over his herd, his nose lifted to the air, sniffing
out danger while he surreptitiously searched for a mare
to mount.

Joanie felt a shiver course through her at the
thought, stunned to find herself silently wishing that
she might be the one he chose.

He continued to stand, his eyes narrowed at the
crowd as if unaware of the eyes directed his way, but
then he slowly turned and looked straight at Joanie, as
if drawn by her gaze. Her heart slammed against her
rib cage as his blue eyes met her green ones across
the smoke-filled room—his dark, almost piercing in

their intensity, hers burning in embarrassment at being caught staring. But as hard as she willed herself otherwise, she couldn't look away. As she watched, he turned and made his way through the crowd toward her table.

"Oh, my stars, he's walking in this direction," Serena whispered under her breath, then muffled a squeal. "And he's headed straight for you!" She slapped a hand on Joanie's arm, her fingernails digging into her friend's flesh. "If you whip out pictures of the twins and scare this man off like you have every other man who's found the courage to approach this table, I swear I'll have you committed myself."

Before Joanie had a chance to respond to Serena's threat, J.D. was at their table, nodding a greeting to both women, but returning his gaze to Joanie's. His eyes, as sultry as a summer night, brought a warm flush to her cheeks.

"Do I know you?" he asked.

Slow, thick, rich. Even his voice elicited visions of slow, hot sex. Though the line was an old one, when delivered by a pro like J.D., it was forgivable. Even so, Joanie couldn't resist teasing him a little. "I don't know, do you?"

She watched his forehead pucker in a frown as he studied her face. "Damned if I know," he said at last. "But if I do, I must have been drunk if I let a beautiful woman like you get away."

Joanie laughed, glad to know that some things in life never changed and J. D. Cawthon was one of them. He was still as big a flirt as ever. "Do you remember George Hill?" she asked, her eyes twinkling with merriment.

His eyebrows shot up at the name. "Hell, yes, I remember George. Haven't seen that old son of a gun in a month of Sundays." He narrowed an eye, looking at her askance. "Don't tell me you're one of those little fillies whose heart he broke when he up and married a few years back?"

Joanie shook her head, laughing. "Hardly. I'm George's sister, Joanie."

J.D.'s frown deepened. "Joanie?" He stepped back, eyeing her. "You mean that gangly, freckle-faced brat that trailed us like a coon dog from one rodeo to another?"

She nodded her head. "Yep, that's me."

J.D. shook his head while he moved his gaze from the top of her head to the tip of her boots, his smile broadening appreciatively. "Well, honey, you sure did some mighty fine growing up."

Joanie laughed, pleased by the compliment. "Thanks...I think." She felt a nudge on her foot and remembered Serena. "I'm sorry. J.D., I'd like you to meet a friend of mine, Serena Fisher. Serena, this is J. D. Cawthon."

J.D. turned his winning smile on Serena, taking her hand in his and bringing it to his lips. "A pleasure to meet you, ma'am." Serena all but melted at his feet, but J.D. didn't even seem to notice. He returned his gaze to Joanie. "Where is old George now?"

"Wyoming. After he and Gayle married, they bought a ranch and moved up there."

"George leave Texas?" He placed a hand over his heart as if wounded. "Why, that's grounds enough to hang a man for treason."

Joanie laughed. "What's worse is that my parents

moved there, too. They went for a visit, fell in love with the state, came back home and sold their cattle ranch, lock, stock and barrel.''

"And you didn't go with them?"

Joanie shook her head sadly, remembering how difficult the decision to remain in Texas had been for her. She started to tell J.D. that she probably would have moved with them if she hadn't been going through a divorce at the time and struggling to support two children. But she remembered her promise to Serena. "No, I stayed behind."

He nodded his approval. "Right choice." He looked at her a moment longer, studying her so intensely Joanie had to struggle to keep from squirming. "Would you like to dance?" he asked.

The question came out of thin air and caught Joanie totally off guard. *Dance? With J. D. Cawthon? Chest to breasts, groin to grinding groin?* As Joanie remembered, that was the only way he knew how. She had dreamed of dancing with him most of her teenage years, had even acted it out in the privacy of her bedroom with a giant teddy bear who usually sat propped on a slipper chair in her room serving as J.D. But hearing the invitation delivered while she was fully awake and as an adult woman was more than a little disconcerting.

Her stomach did a series of nervous flips while she tried to think of an excuse to gracefully refuse. "Thanks," she finally said, "but I wouldn't want to leave Serena alone."

"Oh, don't worry about me," Serena interjected as she quickly slipped off her stool. "I was just leaving."

"Leaving!" Joanie echoed, her dismay at being left alone with J.D. obvious. "But you can't—"

Serena snagged the straps of her purse and dragged it off the table, silencing Joanie with a warning look. "Didn't I tell you?" she said, smiling sweetly while she lied through her teeth. "I promised my sister, Sylvia, I'd be back by twelve. Give me a call in the morning before you head home," she called over her shoulder.

Her heart pounding against her ribs, Joanie watched her friend vanish into the crowd, feeling very much like a lamb left for slaughter. Slowly, she turned her gaze back to J.D.'s.

A grin tugged at one corner of his mouth. "I hope I didn't scare off your friend."

"Serena? Scared?" The very idea was enough to make Joanie forget her fears—at least for the moment—and laugh. "Hardly."

J.D. nodded toward the tall bar stool Serena had vacated. "Mind if I sit down?"

Joanie waved a hand in invitation, thankful that for the time being he'd apparently forgotten about the dance. "Help yourself."

He angled a hip onto the seat, his thigh brushing against Joanie's. Heat crawled up her leg and settled low in her abdomen. She jerked her gaze to his and found him watching her, as if measuring her reaction. Her face flooded with heat. She inched away, putting more space between them.

J.D. closed the space right back up. "Do you live here in San Antonio?" he asked conversationally.

Joanie's mouth went dry and her mind blank. She didn't know how to make small talk with men, which was why Serena had insisted Joanie accompany her to the Watering Hole that night. Serena was convinced that Joanie needed a little refresher course on dating. But Joanie wasn't ready for this. Not yet. And certainly not with J. D. Cawthon. It was Serena who knew how to talk to men, to flirt and tease. Which was exactly why Joanie was going to murder Serena as soon as she caught up with her again. Imagine, leaving her here by herself and at the mercy of a ladies' man like J. D. Cawthon!

Joanie forced a smile to hide her panic. "No, I live in Liberty Hill. I'm just here for the weekend. How about you?" she asked in return.

He shook his head, smiling. "Nah. San Antonio's too big for me. I've got a place near Taylor. I'm just here on business." He rested his forearms on the small circular table and edged closer until their shoulders almost touched. The space between them all but crackled with electricity. He cocked his head toward her, his lips curving in a sensual smile. "But tonight is strictly pleasure," he added with a wink. His mouth was so close, his breath feathered warm and moist against Joanie's cheek.

She had dreamed of moments like this when she was a teenager—she and J.D. all cozied up together like lovers. As an adult woman, she'd even dredged up those dreams from her teenage years to help ward off loneliness in the long, solitary nights after her husband had left her. But those dreams had done nothing to prepare her for the real thing. Not knowing what to say or what to do, Joanie plucked the straw from her drink. Country music pulsed around them, intoxicating in its lusty pull. Unconsciously, she drummed the song's beat on the tabletop while her feet tapped out the bass against the stool's lowest rung.

"How about that dance?" J.D. asked.

Joanie glanced toward the dance floor with longing, her fingers and feet going still. "Oh, I don't know," she replied hesitantly. "I haven't danced the Texas two-step in longer than I can remember."

"Where've you been, a convent?" Before she could answer, he spun off the stool and to his feet. He held out his hand. "It's like riding a horse. You never forget."

Joanie caught her lower lip between her teeth as she glanced at his hand, tempted, but not wanting to make a fool of herself. She'd been married for eight years, divorced for two. She'd been out of the dating game longer than she'd ever been in. And this was J. D. Cawthon, the man of her dreams. She didn't think she could bear it if she made a fool of herself in front of him. She lifted her gaze to his, ready to tell him thanks but no thanks.

But when her eyes met his, the refusal died on her lips. His eyes were the deepest of blues and about as close to bedroom eyes as a man could get. At the moment, they were full of the devil and lit with just enough sexual teasing to make her remember why she had come to the Watering Hole in the first place.

With her children at their grandparents for the weekend, Serena had insisted that Joanie needed to take advantage of this rare opportunity and kick up her heels and have a good time. And so what if it was J. D. Cawthon whom she was having that good time with? she asked herself. She wasn't thirteen now. She was a woman. And the five years that separated them in age no longer seemed such a gap.

Drawing in a deep breath for courage, she laid her hand across his palm. "You asked for it," she warned as she scooted off the stool.

J.D. chuckled, closing his fingers around hers, then tucking her arm beneath his as he led her out to the dance floor. "Yes, ma'am, I believe I did." At the edge of the dance floor, he stopped and wrapped an arm around her waist. His gaze on hers, a teasing smile on his lips, he drew her close until his belt buckle grazed her midriff.

Groin to grinding groin, she remembered, then promptly lost her breath when he spun around, dancing her in a tight exhilarating circle.

If asked later, she couldn't have explained it if she'd tried, but for some reason, a woman who hadn't danced in over ten years was suddenly Ginger Rogers to J.D.'s Fred Astaire. Her body blended with his every movement as if they were one, just as it had in the dreams of her youth when she'd whirled around her bedroom with the giant teddy bear she'd secretly named J.D. She matched his every step, responding to each twirl, each pass under his arm, laughing like a love-struck teenager during a night out on the town. When the song ended, he twirled her in a fast pirouette, then bent her backward over his arm.

Breathless, almost drunk with the excitement of dancing with J.D., Joanie dropped back her head and laughed...then slowly sobered as she watched his face descend toward hers. She knew without a shadow of a doubt that he was going to kiss her.

Did he remember kissing her before? she wondered.

That night a lifetime ago when he'd successfully ridden the bronc that had won him the title of National Champion? As luck would have it, Joanie had been standing behind the chutes that night in Las Vegas waiting for her brother George to gather his equipment when J.D. had swung through the gate. Pumped after his victory, he'd grabbed the eighteen-year-old Joanie, swung her around and around, plastered a bone-melting kiss on her...then strolled away, walking right out of her life without once looking back.

But Joanie had never forgotten. She'd carried the memory with her for more than ten years.

She closed her eyes at the first touch of his lips on hers, absorbing the shock as the familiar arc of lightning shot through her body. A sigh flowed from her to him as she gave herself up to the heat of his lips and feasted on the sensual flavors she found there. Pleasure pearled like thick honey low in her abdomen.

When he drew away, she opened her eyes and found him watching her, a frown gathered between his brows. Had she done something wrong? she wondered, her panic returning with a vengeance. Had she breached some unwritten rule of etiquette in allowing him to kiss her?

He levered her to her feet, then pressed a hand to her lower back and guided her to their table. Joanie climbed up on the bar stool, half-expecting J.D. to thank her for the dance and move on.

Instead, he settled on the stool next to her. He picked up her left hand and tilted it toward the light. "Married?"

Pleased that for whatever reason he wasn't leaving

just yet, Joanie felt the heat rise to flush her cheeks. "Once, to Josh Summers. But I'm divorced now."

He lowered her hand, but kept it in his, closing his fingers around her palm. "Good. I make it a policy not to mess with another man's wife."

"Oh?" Joanie replied, trying not to laugh at his audacity. "And you're planning on messing with me?"

J.D. grinned. "I sure as hell intend to try." He lifted a hand to signal a passing waitress. Dressed in denim short shorts, red cowboy boots and a bandanna crop top that revealed a generous view of cleavage, the young woman quickly cut a swath through the constantly churning crowd and sidled up to J.D., balancing a tray on the palm of one hand. He looped an arm around the waitress's waist, then turned to Joanie. "What's your pleasure?"

His easy way with the woman only confirmed Joanie's suspicions...J. D. Cawthon was as much a playboy as he'd ever been. "A margarita, on the rocks, no salt."

"A lady who knows her mind," he said and winked. "I like that." He tipped his head to the waitress and charmed her with a smile. "And I'll have whatever's on tap." He released the woman and turned his attention fully on Joanie. "So, you're not married," he continued, picking up the last threads of their conversation. "Anyone at home who'd be missing you about now?"

Joanie laughed and shook her head. "No, just..." She started to mention her children, then remembered Serena's warning. There was no reason to mention the twins, she told herself. Knowing J.D., he wouldn't be around long enough to meet them anyway. "A cat," she said instead. "And I doubt that she's missing me."

J.D.'s grin broadened. "Good." He spun on the stool until his knees bumped Joanie's. The earth shifted then settled around her at the contact. Before she had a chance to fully regain her balance, he caught her hands in his and pulled them to his thighs. After flattening them beneath his, he continued his forward motion to circle her waist with his hands. She saw the kiss coming and braced herself for it. Even at that, the onslaught of sensation that ripped through her melted her bones, leaving her weak and helpless.

His tongue touched her lips first, a brush of coarse velvet at the feminine bow of her upper lip that licked a path of heat from one corner of her mouth to the other before slipping between her parted lips. Corded muscles tensed beneath Joanie's palms, a vivid reminder of where her hands lay. The heat of his body sucked at her, drawing her deeper and deeper into the fire.

"That'll be five seventy-five." A harried hand slapped napkins onto the table. The muffled clink of glass followed as the waitress plopped the drinks they'd ordered on top of the napkins.

J.D. withdrew slowly, his eyes fixed on Joanie's, a slow grin building. Joanie fought just to breathe. Her eyes remained locked on his mouth, on temptation, on lips full and red that glistened with moisture from the shared kiss.

He eased a wallet from his back pocket and, without looking, plucked out a bill, laid it on the woman's tray and said, "Keep the change." Snatching up the money, the waitress slipped the twenty-dollar bill into her cleavage and skedaddled before he could change his mind.

J.D. picked up his beer mug, drank long and deep, then set it back down with a satisfied sigh, his gaze lowering to Joanie's.

"Are you gonna let me buy you breakfast?" His voice, deep and husky, skittered along her nerves.

Joanie fought back a rising tide of nervousness. She might have been out of the dating game for a while, but not so long that she didn't recognize a loaded question when she heard one. "Breakfast?" she repeated uneasily.

"Am I going too fast here?" he asked with a grin. "Yeah, breakfast. You know, the first meal of the day."

Joanie started backpedaling as fast as she could. "Oh, I—I don't know," she stammered.

J.D. chuckled. "Now take it easy," he said, keeping his voice low and soothing. "This isn't a marriage proposal, simply an invitation to breakfast." He caught her hands in his, drawing slow, convincing circles against her palms with the pads of his thumbs. "But if something were to happen between now and breakfast...well, we're both free, over twenty-one and consenting adults, aren't we?"

Though she tried to keep her mind focused on reason, every responsible bone in Joanie's body dissolved under the heat of his blue gaze. She'd spent her entire life doing the right thing— being responsible, sensible, never shirking duty or taking a chance or letting her emotions rule. For once in her life she wanted to touch the flame, grab the brass ring, taste the sweet nectar of temptation. For just one night she wanted to forget that she was a single mother. To hell with responsibility and kids and overdue bills. They'd all still be there Sunday, waiting for her when she returned home. But tonight, just for tonight, she wanted to forget.

And J. D. Cawthon was just the man to make that happen.

Joanie felt all elbows, thumbs and knees as she struggled with the coded card that opened her hotel room. Seeing her difficulties, J.D. eased the card from her hand. "Here, let me," he offered.

Joanie stepped back, immediately knotting her hands at her waist. She'd never felt more inadequate, more out of her league than she did at this moment. And all because of a little thing called inexperience. What she'd give for a five-minute briefing from Serena on the etiquette of a one-night stand.

And that's all this was.

She knew J.D. well enough to know that his record with a woman never lasted longer than one night. Joanie knew that and accepted it, but it certainly didn't put her at ease.

The lock gave and J.D. pushed open the door. No time now for regrets or second thoughts, she realized as he stepped back to let her pass in front of him. Joanie slipped by, smiling, trying her best not to let her nervousness show.

Once inside, though, with the door closed and the bed growing in size by the moment, Joanie felt a fresh wave of panic.

"J.D.," she began hesitantly as she skirted the foot of the bed in order to put some distance between them, "I'm not so sure this is such a good idea."

He cocked his head to look at her, the brow with the scar that ran through it knitted in a frown. "And why is that?" he asked as he tossed the coded card onto the dresser and turned to face her.

Joanie felt heat flood her cheeks. "I don't have much experience at this kind of thing," she explained, her embarrassment growing by the minute. "In fact," she said with a self-conscious laugh, "I've never done anything like this in my entire life. I would imagine a man of your experience would find a night with me a disappointment."

His gaze dropped to her waist where her fingers nervously knotted and unknotted and his blue eyes softened in understanding. He crossed to her, his movements slow and nonthreatening, obviously not wanting to frighten her any more than she already was. Gently, he took her hands in his.

"A disappointment?" He caught a wisp of honey blond hair and tucked it behind her ear, a twinkle sparking to life in his eyes. "Darlin', I can promise you I won't be disappointed." He let his hand slide to cup her jaw. "There are no expectations here. You and me are just two old friends in a strange town looking for a little company and a little pleasure to help pass the night."

He took her hands again and guided them around his waist, then circled her waist with his arms, drawing her closer still. When he dipped his knees to meet her gaze and those blue eyes of his met hers, any misgivings or concerns over experience or the lack thereof dissolved at the heat she found in his eyes. On a sigh, she melted against his chest. "Oh, J.D...." she murmured as his arms closed around her.

There was something so exquisitely right about being in his arms, about the way her head nestled perfectly in the hollowed nook between his shoulder and neck. There was a comfort and security within the span of his arms, something Joanie wasn't sure she'd ever felt with any other man, but something she'd always known would exist between her and J.D.

He shifted slightly, and his head lowered to hers. There was a naturalness, too, in the way their lips meshed, a satisfaction in the blending of flavors, his with hers. But then his tongue slipped between her lips and comfort and rightness were forgotten as that same electrical charge surged through her again. It had happened the very first time ten years ago when he'd kissed her behind the chutes at the rodeo arena in Las Vegas. The years hadn't diminished the impact. Bolts of sensation shot to her every extremity, then ricocheted back to settle in a churning pool of heat low in her abdomen. Joanie had experienced nothing before or since to equal it.

Is this a dream, she asked herself, like so many others that she'd awakened from over the years only to find herself alone? Wanting reassurance, she slipped her arms from his waist and smoothed them up the length of his chest until she framed his face between her hands. His skin was warm beneath her fingertips and very much alive, the muscles in his jaw working as his mouth moved over hers. She traced the crevice of the scar that ran across his cheek and sighed. Yes, this was J.D., the man of her dreams come to life.

Slow and hypnotizing, his hands moved on her as he deepened the kiss, slowly inching the fabric of her broomstick skirt higher and higher up her thighs until his bare hands cupped her buttocks through her silk panties. Once there, he paused, kneading gently at first, teasing her hips into motion until her groin rubbed against his in ever-tightening, provocative circles. The pressure of his fingers increased then, evoking pleasures so rich in sensation that it was all Joanie could do not to sink to her knees.

As if he sensed her weakness, J.D. walked her backward, guiding her with the pressure of his thighs, until her calves bumped the bed. He let her skirt slip back down in place, then smoothed his fingers around her waist in search of the knot that cinched her belt of brightly woven threads. The belt fell at their feet, freeing the over-size denim shirt. J.D.'s hands slipped beneath the voluminous hem, lighting delicious fires as his callused hands skimmed over her skin. In one smooth upward motion, the shirt was over her head and drifting to the floor behind them, leaving Joanie no time for attacks of modesty. Her bra followed and then, and only then, did J.D. move his lips from hers. He stepped back, his hands on her shoulders, holding her in place, and let his gaze move down the length of her.

Fear seized Joanie, tying her stomach in knots. Would he find her attractive? she worried silently, then cursed herself for not thinking to turn out the bedside lamp. Giving birth to twins had changed her body. Her stomach muscles weren't what they used to be, her breasts not quite as high and firm as they'd once been. And if he looked closely, she knew he'd discover the tiny almost translucent stretch marks that traversed her abdomen.

But her worries dissolved beneath the heat of the fingertips he placed at the hollow of her throat. His fingers followed his gaze, almost worshipful in their touch as they dipped over her breast in an agonizing path to her waist.

When he reached her skirt, he dipped his thumbs beneath the elasticized band and skimmed it down her legs, his teeth nipping at her abdomen as he knelt, holding the waist of the skirt open while she stepped free.

Trembling now from desire as much as nerves, Joanie watched as J.D. lifted his gaze to hers. A slow smile crooked at one side of his mouth. "Like I said," he murmured, his voice husky, "you've done some mighty fine growing up."

Heat flooded Joanie's cheeks, embarrassment and pleasure warring for dominance there. He rose slowly, his gaze on hers, dragging his fingers up the length of her legs, dipping them into the curve between her legs, watching the heat build in her green eyes as he stroked. She closed her eyes against the fires he created and sagged against him. "My God, J.D.," she murmured breathlessly, her hands fisted in the bib of his cavalry-style shirt for support. "What are you doing to me?"

His chuckle was low and throaty. "Making love to you, sweetheart. Just making love."

He made it sound so simple, yet there was nothing simple about the way his fingers stroked her, plucking sensations from deep within her and exposing them until they ignited, blazing out of control. Her breath grew shorter and her fingers itched to touch him, as well.

Finding the courage to do just that, she reached for one of the brass buttons on his shirt, her nerve growing with each freed disk. When the last button slipped out, she flipped back the bib and flattened her hands against the expanse of chest revealed. Smoothing her hands upward over the soft mat of hair, she eased the shirt over his shoulders, exposing him fully. A small gasp escaped her lips when she saw the long, jagged scar running the length of his collarbone. Her gaze sought his.

A rueful smile played at one corner of his mouth as he rubbed a self-conscious hand across the scar. "Not very pretty, is it?"

In answer, Joanie pushed his hand away and pressed her lips against the puckered flesh, saddened that she hadn't always been around to make her deals with God to keep J.D. safe from the bronc's razor-sharp hooves. His low moan of approval vibrated against her lips, renewing her urgency to explore.

She heard the clink of metal as J.D. loosened the silver buckle at his waist and joined her hands with his in a frantic race to work open the buttons that closed his fly. Whispering promises of the pleasure to come, J.D. eased her onto the bed and followed her, toeing off his boots. His lips found hers again as he wriggled his way out of his jeans and kicked them to the floor. Within seconds, heated flesh met heated flesh as he stretched to match his body down the length of hers.

The sensation was both satisfying and frustrating. A woman who'd spent the past two years living a nun-like existence, Joanie suddenly yearned for more. She shifted beneath him, spreading her legs, offering him access.

"Hold on a second," he said, his own anxiousness apparent in the huskiness of his voice. "I need to grab some protection.'' He stretched an arm over the side of the bed and reached for his jeans.

''It's okay,'' Joanie murmured. ''I'm protected.''

He hesitated a second longer, studying her, then dropped the jeans to the floor and turned back to her. On a sigh, he eased the lower part of his body between her thighs.

With fifteen years of unfulfilled dreams feeding her desire for J.D., Joanie opened for him, drawing him in, moaning her pleasure to at last feel the strength of him, the sheer power centered in that part of him that eased inside her. She moved against him, wanting every centimeter of pleasure, cherishing every nuance of sensation his throbbing flesh offered. His skin grew slick with perspiration beneath her hands as she sought to draw him closer still.

Her eyes open, unwilling to lose sight of him for even a second for fear he'd disappear again in the clouds of a dream, Joanie watched the storm build within him—the tightening of his facial muscles, eyes squeezed shut against the razor-sharp pleasure slicing through him, the trembling in his limbs. The storm raged on until it held him helpless in its grip...and she knew a power that she'd never known before.

''Come on, J.D.,'' she urged breathlessly, arching her hips against his, meeting his every hungry thrust. ''Take me with you.''

The growl erupted from deep inside him, some wild place Joanie yearned to explore. He tossed back his head and sank his fingers into the tender flesh of her buttocks as he pulled her against him, burying himself deep inside her. Her throat closed around an indrawn breath as the pressure inside her built to an almost unbearable crescendo. Then she felt herself falling,

falling, spiraling out of control, and she grabbed for him, her fingers tangling in the hair on his chest. He clenched his teeth against the shudders that racked his body as they both let the pleasure take them.

Slowly, his chest expanding beneath her spread hands, he hauled in one last shaky breath, then dipped his chin to meet her gaze. Glazed with heat, his blue eyes bored into hers and Joanie felt she'd been branded as clearly as if a hot iron had touched her flesh…and knew that as long as she lived, she'd never forget this night, nor this man.

On a groan, he collapsed against her, curling his arms around her and rolling while keeping their bodies joined, until he rested beneath her and Joanie lay snuggled against his chest. "Joanie…Joanie…Joanie…" he murmured against her hair.

She kissed his chin, the hollow at his neck, then tucked a hand beneath her cheek, her lips curving in a wistful smile over his heart. She'd never known such pleasure, nor experienced such passion.

But she also knew that when morning came and they parted, J.D. would give her a kiss and send her on her way without any promises, without a backward glance. That was his way, part of the mystique that made him so attractive to women.

Her eyes misted and she closed them against the tears. As much as she wished otherwise, Joanie knew that their parting wouldn't be as easy for her. She had carried him around in her dreams and in her heart for so long that he was a part of her.

And now that her dream had taken life, she knew forgetting him would be impossible.

Chapter Two

Two months later

Joanie sat in a booth in Mavis's Café, staring blindly at the hairlike threads springing from a tiny split in the worn, brown vinyl bench opposite her. Except for a state trooper, who sat on a stool at the serving counter nursing his afternoon cup of coffee, she had the place to herself. From the kitchen, a radio played, the canned voice of a newsman droning out the afternoon farm report. Mavis herself stood behind the counter, refilling salt and pepper shakers during the lull between lunch and dinner.

Overhead, a ceiling fan hummed, its wooden blades chopping the air, the breeze it stirred the only relief from the oppressive June heat the window air conditioner didn't stand a prayer of defeating. In spite of the heat, Joanie huddled over her hot cup of coffee, chilled to the bone, her skin dotted with goose bumps. Through thoughts that remained jumbled and unfocused, she sought desperately to find the answer to one lone question.

What was she going to do now?

She fought to stifle the sob that rose in her throat. It burned deep and savage low in her throat. A single woman, divorced, the mother of five-year-old twins, who supported herself and her children by teaching at the local high school, pregnant? Oh, God, what was she going to do?

She folded her arms on the table and dropped her head. She'd known the truth before she'd made the appointment with Doc Reynolds to confirm it. Birth control pills proved effective in ninety-seven percent of the female population, Doc had told her. Unfortunately, it appeared Joanie Summers fell somewhere in that ineffective three percent range.

And didn't it just figure? she thought morosely. One lousy night, one little tumble in the face of temptation and she wound up pregnant. Sighing, she lifted her head, scraping the heels of her hands beneath her eyes. Tears wouldn't do her any good now, she told herself. She had decisions to make.

For Joanie, there was no such thing as an unwanted child. There were unexpected, maybe even unwanted pregnancies, but never an unwanted child. For her, abortion or adoption were not options worthy of consideration. She had a responsibility to the baby to give it life and all the love and care it deserved.

But what about the baby's father? she wondered further. What were her responsibilities to him?

An image of J. D. Cawthon formed in her mind and with it a want throbbed to life deep within her. Heat flooded her cheeks as a molten softness spread slowly through her abdomen. Two months had passed since she'd spent the night with him in San Antonio and still the mere thought of him turned her insides to putty.

Giving herself a shake, she pushed the distracting thoughts away to focus on her responsibilities to J.D. in this matter. She supposed it was her duty to inform him that he was about to become a father. Not that she wanted or expected anything from him. She didn't. But she did feel the choice and level of his involvement in the child's life was his to make, not hers.

Sighing, she angled her face toward the window that looked out on the main street that ran through the town of Liberty Hill. A small town with small-town values. She wasn't sure how the school board would respond to the news of her pregnancy. Would they ask for her resignation? A stupid question, she chided silently. Of course they would, and if they didn't, she'd resign anyway. What kind of example would she be setting for an impressionable group of teenagers? Not that giving up her job wouldn't hurt, but she was a grown woman and responsible for her actions.

Responsible. Yes, she was responsible all right. Had always been so. Except for that one weekend two months ago. If only…

She shook herself, refusing to deal with if onlys. What she would deal with were the facts, and the fact was she was pregnant.

The cowbell over the café's front door clanged as the door opened. Joanie glanced up, then froze, unconsciously dropping a hand to her abdomen as she watched a man step inside and pause as he let the door squeak shut behind him.

J. D. Cawthon? What in the world was he doing in Liberty Hill? Was this some kind of cruel joke God was playing on her? She hadn't seen or heard from J.D. once in the two months since she'd spent the night with him, and now, less than an hour after she discovers that she's pregnant with his child, he strolls into Mavis's Café? The irony was almost more than she could bear.

He glanced around, obviously looking for a waitress to direct him to a table when his gaze lit on Joanie. His eyebrows shot up and a slow grin of recognition spread across his face. He dragged off his hat, hooked it over a peg by the door and strode toward her booth, finger combing his hair into place.

"Well, if this isn't my lucky day." He slid onto the bench opposite hers, still grinning. "I was just thinking about you."

Her face felt starched, the skin threatening to crack as she forced a smile in return. "Were you?"

His grin softened, taking on a seductive edge as he leaned closer. "I was going to call you later, after I took care of some business, to see if you had plans for tonight."

Really? How fortunate, because I was just thinking of calling you, too. You see, I wanted to inform you that in approximately seven months you're going to be a father.

Her stomach pitched, rolled, then settled as she pictured his reaction. The announcement would probably bring on a heart attack. No, she couldn't tell him so bluntly and certainly not in a place as public as the café. Besides, the information was too new, too painful to even consider sharing. Later, she promised herself. She'd tell him later after she'd had time to accept the news of the pregnancy herself. She opened her purse and quickly counted out change to cover the price of the coffee.

"I'm sorry, but I already have plans. In fact," she said with a quick glance at her wristwatch, "I'm late for an appointment now." She jerked the strap of her purse over her shoulder and pushed out of the booth. She tried another smile. This one was even more painful than the last. "It was nice seeing you again, J.D." she murmured, then spun and headed for the exit.

J.D. sat in the booth and watched Joanie leave, his eyebrows drawn together in a frown. If he wasn't mistaken, he'd just received the royal brush-off. And that didn't settle well with him at all. Not that he hadn't been turned down by a woman before. He had. But in the past it had always been from women who he hadn't known were either married or engaged and the rejection was always delivered in a kindly manner and with real regret. Nothing at all like the rejection he'd just received from Joanie. She certainly hadn't given him the brush-off two months before when they'd met at that dance hall in San Antonio. Then, she'd been primed and willing, and he'd bet his prize mare that she'd enjoyed that night as much as he had.

And he had enjoyed the night with her. Maybe a little too much, he remembered, his frown deepening. A day hadn't passed since that he hadn't thought about her. Several times he'd considered calling her, but each time something would come up, diverting him in another direction. A mare would deliver a new colt or a stallion would tear down a fence or bust out of a stall.

When he'd heard about the stud for sale at the Potts farm in Liberty Hill, he'd immediately thought of Joanie, remembering she lived there, as well. He'd meant to call her days ago and set up a date in advance, but somehow the time had gotten away from him.

And now here he sat, his plans for a tumble in the hay with Joanie quickly going up in smoke. He caught himself just shy of feeling sorry for himself. *And since when did J. D. Cawthon let a little "no" stand between him and a good time?* he asked himself. He stood and stuffed his shirttail a little more neatly in the waist of jeans.

By golly, plans can be changed, he told himself as he strode toward the door. He plucked his hat from the peg and settled it on his head, aligning the brim carefully with the weight of one finger.

He hadn't driven fifty miles for nothing but taking delivery on a prime piece of horseflesh. He was going to see Joanie Summers and persuade her to change those plans and spend the evening with him...and maybe the night. A smile broadened on his face. He'd certainly do his part to make that change of plans worth her while.

He sauntered over to the counter and offered the woman behind the register one of his most charming smiles. "Ma'am," he said politely, "could I trouble you for the use of your telephone directory?"

Mavis all but fell off her stool in her haste to drag

the book out from under the counter. J.D. accepted it from her with the calm assurance of a man accustomed to getting what he wanted from women.

"Thank you, ma'am," he said with a wink, making her sigh. "I'm obliged."

Joanie poured a cup of water over Trevor's head and watched tiredly as he raised his shoulders to his ears, squealing as the shampoo suds streamed down his face.

"Uh-uh," she warned, placing a restraining hand over Trey's before he could shovel another load of bubbles onto the top of his twin brother's head. "We-'re washing the soap out, not putting more in."

The doorbell sounded and she leaned back to yell through the partially opened bathroom door. "Marissa! Marissa, honey, will you see who's at the door?" She listened a moment, waiting for her daughter's answering call. When none was forthcoming, she rocked back on her heels and dragged Trevor from the bath. The bell sounded again. "I'm coming," she called, then quickly wrapped a towel around Trevor. Grabbing another towel, she wound it around Trey and lifted him dripping into her arms. With an order for Trevor to follow, she hurried to the door. Trevor trotted after them, naked as the day he was born, dragging his towel behind him.

She opened the door and just managed to stifle a frustrated moan when she saw J.D. standing there, wearing a smile as big as his Stetson. His gaze dipped from hers to the toddler in her arms, then farther down to the naked toddler at her side. His smile slowly melted into a look of sheer terror.

His one-word question came out on a hoarse croak. "Yours?"

If Joanie had harbored any doubts of J.D.'s feelings for kids, his reaction to the twins would have resolved it right then and there. Joanie was tempted to tell him yes, the boys were hers, suspecting that nothing would scare off J. D. Cawthon faster than a woman burdened with a passel of kids, but a natural honesty made her heave a sigh. She shifted the toddler to a more comfortable position on her hip. "No, a friend's. I'm baby-sitting."

His relief was obvious in the relaxing of his shoulders and the release of his pent-up breath, proving to Joanie that she'd been correct in her assumption. His grin slipped back into place. "I hope not for long," he replied. "I was hoping I could talk you into having dinner with me tonight."

"I'm sorry, J.D., but really, I can't. I—"

At that moment, the back door slammed and Marissa came screaming through the house. "Mommy! Mommy! Come quick! Shane's stuck up in the tree!"

J.D.'s gaze shifted to the newest arrival. *Mommy?* Was this little girl Joanie's? Before he could voice the question, Joanie thrust the toddler she held into his arms and took off like a shot for the back of the house in hot pursuit of Marissa. J.D. held the child at arm's length, as if he'd been handed a live grenade.

The little boy just grinned at him. With a shudder, J.D. turned to follow Joanie, but then the second little guy, the mirror image of the one he was holding, started crying, stopping him in his tracks. J.D. frowned at the second toddler for a minute, then shifted the one he already held to a football carry under one arm and scooped the other twin from the floor and settled him in the same fashion under the opposite arm...and prayed the two rugrats were housebroken. His jaw set in determination, he took off in the direction Joanie had taken.

He found her in the backyard, one foot braced against the trunk of a tree, hopping on the other as she stretched to grab hold of a limb that was just out of reach. High above her, a little boy clung to a swaying branch. J.D. centered his gaze on the boy, already plotting the easiest path through the branches to reach him as he pressed the toddlers into Joanie's arms. "Here. I'll get the kid down."

Relieved to be rid of the little ones, he quickly hefted himself up into the fork of the tree's trunk, then climbed his way slowly toward the boy.

"Hey there, little guy," he said, forcing his voice to remain calm. "I'm going to get you down in just a jiffy. Can you inch yourself backward on that limb? Good job," he said, when the boy started moving backward with the slow, measured movements of an inchworm. When the boy was within reach, J.D. locked an arm around the kid's waist and plucked him from the branch. "Now you just wrap your arms around my neck and we'll climb down together, okay, cowboy?"

"My name's Shane," the boy replied, sniffling.

"Used to have an old cow dog by the name of Shane," J.D. told the boy, hoping to keep the child's mind off the dangerous climb down the tree.

"Really?" Shane asked, his eyes round with curiosity.

"Yep. Best herding dog I ever owned." J.D. felt

his boot slide into the fork of the tree's trunk and his cheeks puffed in a sigh of relief. He leaned to pass Shane into his mother's waiting arms. Joanie grabbed her son, crushing him to her chest.

His mission completed, J.D. started to jump down when Marissa called out, "Hey, mister! You forgot my kitty."

J.D. looked back up into the tree branches, noticing for the first time the kitten crouched on one of the tree's upper limbs.

He offered Marissa one of his most charming and hopefully convincing smiles. "Don't you worry your pretty little head about that kitten. Cats love to climb trees and know all the best ways to climb back down."

Marissa didn't buy his story for a second. She swelled up and started bawling like a lost calf in a hailstorm. The sound clawed its way up J.D.'s spine and worked on his last good nerve. "I want my kitty," she wailed pitifully.

Before he thought better of it, J.D. was heading back up that tree trunk. "It's okay, sweetie," he soothed. "You don't need to cry anymore. J.D.'ll get your kitty down." He grabbed ahold of a limb and levered himself higher, mumbling under his breath, "Damn fool cat. Gonna get both our necks broke."

When he reached the limb where the cat was perched, he lowered himself to his stomach, and shimmied out onto the branch.

"Here, kitty, kitty, kitty," he called in a singsongy voice. The kitten simply stared at him unblinkingly, his eyes looking like glass marbles, the hair on his neck raised. J.D. stretched his hand out, ready to grab the kitten by the scruff of the neck and haul it back down that tree but fast, when the kitten suddenly leaped, sinking its claws into J.D.'s neck and shoulders.

Caught off guard, J.D. yelped in pain, then lost his grip on the limb and fell, hurtling through the mesh of leaf-covered branches like a comet from space. Limbs snapped beneath his weight, scraping against his flesh while the kitten kept a clawhold on his neck. Just before they hit the ground, the kitten jumped free, landing on its feet a good six feet from J.D.

J.D. felt something snap in his left leg and almost cried out at the pain. With the breath knocked out of him, it took him a few seconds before he was able to push himself to his elbows and try to sit up. His gaze landed on the kitten who sat nearby calmly licking its paws. Twisting his lips in a snarl at the blasted cat, he tried to roll to his feet. Pain knifed through his leg, draining the blood from his face and the strength from his body. He fell back with a groan.

Joanie rushed to his side. "Are you all right?" she cried, her voice rising in hysteria.

J.D. clamped his teeth together as she laid a hand on his injured leg. "Please," he managed to grate out. "Don't touch my leg."

Joanie snatched her hand back. "I won't, I promise." She scooted nearer his head, laying a motherly hand on his forehead. "Do you think it's broken?" At his white-lipped nod, she asked, "Do you want me to call for an ambulance?"

Though he wished with all his heart he could pull himself to his feet and walk away from this house and Joanie Summers and her kids and forget he'd ever even considered stopping by and trying to talk her into a rerun of their last night together in San Antonio, he knew that was impossible.

"Maybe you better," he muttered, closing his eyes against the pain and the humiliation and the five sets of eyes peering down at him.

It took Joanie almost two hours to load up her friend Jane Ellen's twin boys, take them home, apologize for having to cut short Jane Ellen's evening of freedom, then make the trip to the hospital in Georgetown to check on J.D. The entire time she worried about him, keeping the needle of the speedometer on his twin-cab truck hovering on the legal limit while at the same time keeping a cautious eye on the horse trailer she pulled behind her and the wild-eyed stallion inside. She felt responsible that J.D. had broken his leg falling out of her tree and felt guiltier still that she'd been forced to send him off in the ambulance alone.

She should have saved her worries for someone who needed them.

When she reached the emergency room, breathless, dragging two cranky five-year-olds kicking and screaming behind her, she found J.D. surrounded by a flock of nurses who were fussing over him as if he was the only patient they had. He lay propped on a pillow on the hospital gurney, his leg already sporting a plaster cast, sipping an iced cola, his free arm draped around the waist of a pretty redhead while he entertained them all with stories of his "old bronc-riding days."

When he glanced up and saw Joanie standing in the doorway, the smile melted off his face, drawing the gazes of the nurses to Joanie, as well. They must have mistaken the look of disgust on her face as the expression of a jealous wife because they quickly remembered other duties and slipped past Joanie faster than hot butter can pass through a sieve.

J.D. scowled. "What are you doing here?" he asked irritably.

"I came to take you home."

"I can take myself," he muttered gruffly.

She arched a brow his way, looking pointedly at his cast. "And you're planning on driving your truck? The one you left parked in front of my house? The one with a stick shift in the floor and a clutch that's stiffer than the plaster on that cast?"

J.D. looked at her suspiciously, his scowl darkening. "How do you know my clutch is stiff?"

"I noticed it on the way over here. Now—"

"You drove my truck!" he roared, pushing himself to a sitting position. Pain shot up his thigh at the movement and he groaned falling back against the pillows.

"Yes, I drove your truck," she replied. "I couldn't very well leave it parked at my house indefinitely with that horse in the trailer." She saw the look of concern flash in his eyes at the mention of the horse. "Don't worry," she hurried to assure him. "Your horse is fine. I fed and watered him before I drove over here."

"Are you crazy?" J.D. cried. "That horse weighs almost two thousand pounds and is as high-strung as they come. He could've killed you!"

"Well, he didn't, did he?" She peeked around the curtained wall. "Now where did those nurses disappear to? We need to see about getting you released."

* * *

J.D. rode the entire fifty miles back to his farm in tight-lipped silence, his leg throbbing within the cast like a mare in heat, his male ego in tatters. He'd been outmaneuvered by a wisp of a woman who obviously had written the book on bossy. Without asking his permission, she'd parked her two kids in a chair by his bed in the emergency room, instructing them that they weren't to move so much as a hair but were to stay put and keep an eye on J.D. Then she had disappeared.

He had monitored her movements beyond the curtained wall by following the sound of her voice, straining to listen while she consulted with the doctor on the care of his leg. *His* leg, mind you! She'd returned moments later with J.D.'s release papers tucked under her arm, swinging a sack containing the medications for pain the doctor had prescribed and dragging a pair of crutches behind her.

A male nurse had followed her, pushing a wheelchair. Blustering the entire time that he didn't need the damn wheelchair, that he could walk to the truck himself, J.D. was bodily lifted from the bed to the chair by this hulk of a nurse and whisked from the emergency room and out onto a loading platform where Joanie had parked his truck.

And now here he was, a plaster cast running from midthigh to his toes, being chauffeured in his own damn truck by a woman. Frowning, he stole a glance over his shoulder to the seat behind him where Joanie's kids slept, tangled together like a pair of exhausted puppies after a romp in a field. Esmerelda, the kitten he'd rescued from the tree, lay curled on their entwined legs. His frown deepened. It was all their fault. If the boy hadn't chased that damn fool cat up the tree and if the girl hadn't pitched such a fit for him to get it down, J.D. wouldn't have been in the damn tree in the first place.

"Is this the turnoff?" Joanie asked, interrupting his pity party for one.

"Yeah," he mumbled. He lifted a hand as the truck bumped over the cattle guard and pointed. "The stud barn's over there. Stop in front of the double doors so I can unload."

Joanie turned in the direction he indicated, eased to a stop in front of the barn and shut off the engine. When J.D. started to open his door, she stretched a hand across the seat to stop him. He snapped his head around to glare at her and their eyes met across the length of the seat. "You can't manage with that cast," she told him gently. "I'll unload the horse."

"Like hell you will," he muttered at her back as she climbed down from the truck. He swung open his door, grabbed one of the crutches and snugged it under his armpit. Every step was torture, the throbbing in his leg increasing until he was almost blinded by the pain, but he refused to let a woman do his work.

At the rear of the trailer, he shouldered a surprised Joanie out of his way and slipped the lock, swinging open the door and letting down the ramp. The crutch only hampered his movements as he climbed the ramp and he tossed it aside in frustration. Inside the trailer, the powerful horse danced sideways, throwing his head and snorting at the unfamiliar scents and noises around him, nervous after being confined for so long.

J.D. moved to the door at the horse's head, talking

to him in a low voice while he eased his way through the opening and wrapped the lead rope twice around his hand. Clucking softly, he urged the stallion backward, gently guiding him down the ramp and out into the night air. But once the stud's shoulders cleared the trailer and he realized he was free of the trailer's confining walls, he reared, jerking J.D. off his feet. J.D. hit the ground with a jarring thump and bit back a curse as the leg with the cast twisted beneath him. Gritting his teeth against the pain, he clung to the rope, the rough hemp burning his hands, while the horse reared, churning dirt. Clods of earth stung his face and choking dust filled his nose and throat.

He caught a glimpse of movement out of the corner of his eye. "Get back," he yelled when he realized it was Joanie. She ignored him. She kept coming, her hand outstretched, her voice even as she spoke to the horse, trying to distract him while she placed herself between J.D. and the horse's churning hooves.

When the stallion caught her scent, he jerked his head upward, his eyes rolling in fear as he lunged backward, almost sitting on his haunches. Joanie leaped at him and caught the lead rope below his chin and hung on for dear life, using all her weight to keep the horse's head down to prevent him from rearing again.

Drawing on his remaining strength, J.D. rolled to his good knee. His chest heaving, he half dragged himself, half crawled to the corral gate. Using the iron rails like a ladder, he hauled himself to his feet, holding himself erect against the corral fence as he slid the metal glide back and shoved open the gate.

"Joanie, over here," he gasped. "Lead him over here."

Digging her heels into the tightly packed earth in order to keep from being jerked off her feet, Joanie managed to keep a grip around the stud's halter as she tugged him in the direction of the corral. Once inside the gate, though, she quickly clicked free the clasp on the lead rope, then leaped to safety as J.D. swung the gate closed behind her and slid the lock into place. The horse reared, his hooves clawing the night air, then bolted, charging around the corral, looking for a way of escape.

J.D. and Joanie both sagged against the gate, fighting for breath.

"You're crazy, you know that, don't you?" he managed to say, his breath still coming in deep, heaving gasps.

Joanie turned her head toward him, her legs still trembling from the scare she'd received when she had seen J.D. go down in front of the stallion's hooves. She pushed a lock of hair from her face to better see him, her hands shaking after the effort of matching strength with the powerful stallion, but needing the reassurance that J.D. was in fact safe.

In the glow from the security light over the barn, she could see his face, pale beneath the dirt that streaked it, his lips compressed against the pain...and knew that her heart belonged to this man. Unbeknownst to him, she had lost it to him years before and only just realized that she had never fully reclaimed it.

"Anybody who'd even take the time to try to save your ornery hide would have to be," she muttered, needing to hide her true emotions from him. Lifting his arm, she slung it around her shoulders, then slipped her arm around his waist, offering herself as a human crutch as she helped him hobble back to the truck.

Joanie stood outside the bathroom, her ear pressed to the door, listening, ready to bust her way in if she heard anything even remotely out of the ordinary. She had already done a quick check of the house and had decided there was no way J.D. could manage on his own for the next week until the swelling in his leg went down enough to change his cast to a walking one.

Navigating the many steps in the split-level house would be dangerous, but considering the Mexican-tile floors and their characteristically uneven surface, walking with crutches might also prove treacherous. To further convince herself she couldn't leave him alone, a search through the kitchen had turned up nothing more nutritious than a stale package of tortillas, a six-pack of beer and an unopened can of beer nuts.

"Is there anyone I can call to come and take care of you?" she called through the door.

She heard the lid drop and the commode flush and what she was sure was a frustrated sigh. "No, but I'll be fine," he said, his reply muffled. "I have a couple who work for me and they'll look after me."

"Where are they?"

Water splashed into the sink. "They're in Mexico visiting Lupe's parents. I'll just give 'em a call and tell 'em they need to get back home."

The water shut off and the door opened. J.D. hobbled out, his hands braced on the door frame for support. If anything, washing his face had served only to emphasize its paleness. Joanie slipped under his shoulder and threw an arm around his waist. "Let's get you settled in bed," she suggested gently, "then we'll make that call." When he didn't offer any arguments, Joanie realized the extent of his pain.

She wobbled down the hall, taking more and more of his weight. In his room, she helped him cross to the bed, then waited while he hopped on one foot and twisted around before dropping awkwardly to the covers. He fell back with a weary sigh and closed his eyes.

She slipped out of the room, took a detour to check on the twins in the den where they were watching television and then went on to the kitchen for a glass of water and one of the pain pills the doctor had prescribed. When she returned to the bedroom, J.D. was where she'd left him, one arm slung across his eyes, the other cradling the portable phone against his chest.

"J.D.?" she whispered.

He raised his arm and lifted his head a fraction to peer at her through bleary eyes. She set the glass and pill on the nightstand, then took the phone from his chest and replaced it on its base.

"Did you get in touch with them?" she asked as she held out her arm. He curled his fingers around it, using her weight to pull himself to a sitting position.

"No. Phone service down there isn't too reliable." He scooped up the pill, popped it into his mouth and grimaced at the bitter taste before washing it down with the water. "But I'll get through," he added as he leaned over to push the glass onto the nightstand.

While Joanie watched, he ripped open his shirt,

pearlized snaps popping, and shrugged out of it. His shoulders drooped in exhaustion and he let the shirt drop to the floor. Then he fell back on the bed as if even that much effort was more than he had to spare.

Feeling sorry for him, Joanie picked up his good foot and tugged off his boot. Her nails scraped the arch of his foot as she stripped off his sock and she felt him tense against her hands before he dragged his foot from her grasp.

"You don't have to do this," he mumbled gruffly. "I can undress myself."

Hoping to put him more at ease, she teased, "And rob me of the pleasure of taking advantage of a helpless man?"

"I'm not helpless," he denied, then rose to his feet to prove it. In his haste, he put a little too much pressure on his bad leg and the pain had him sagging back down.

"J.D.," she asked softly, "do you want me to help you with your pants?"

When he offered no argument, she reached for his belt buckle, unhooked it, then worked open the buttons down his fly. Since the staff at the hospital had already split high the seam of his jeans that covered the leg with the cast, peeling his pants off wasn't difficult. The hard part was making her fingers behave and keeping her eyes on the job at hand.

Once she had him under the covers and a stack of pillows beneath his leg to help with the swelling, she breathed a sigh of relief.

She stooped to pick up his jeans from the floor and J.D.'s hand stopped her. "I appreciate what you've done for me, Joanie," he said, his tongue already thick from the effects of the pain medication. He dropped his hand. "But please, take your kids and go home. I'll send Manuel for my truck when he and Lupe return."

Joanie hesitated. She knew that he didn't want her there—he'd made that more than evident—but she couldn't bring herself to leave. Not when there was no one nearby to check on him. What if he fell while trying to make his way to the bathroom and wasn't able to get to the phone to call for help? No, she couldn't leave, but how in the world was she ever going to convince him to let her stay?

"J.D.," she began, then saw that his eyes were closed. She tiptoed closer. "J.D.?" she called softly. When he didn't respond, she called a little louder, "J.D." When he still didn't respond, she smiled, knowing the pain pills had kicked in.

J.D. awoke, feeling a strong call of nature. He tossed off the sheet and started to roll out of bed, then winced when the weight of the cast stopped him. He groaned and fell back against the pillow, remembering.

"Do you need to make pee-pee?" a little voice asked.

J.D. whipped his head around. There in a chair pulled next to his bed sat Marissa, Joanie's daughter.

He caught the sheet and jerked it to his chin. "What are you doing here?" he demanded angrily. "I thought y'all went home."

"Mama and Shane did. But Mama left me so I could keep an eye on you."

"She did what!" J.D. roared.

Marissa jumped at the tone of his voice and her bottom lip quivered.

"Oh, for crying out loud!" he exclaimed, his mood turning more sour by the second. "You're not gonna start bawling again like some kinda crybaby, are you?"

Marissa's chin came up and J.D. saw with relief that she'd inherited her mother's spunk. "I'm not a crybaby."

"Good. Now explain to me where your mother went and why she left you here."

"She went home to get us some clothes so we could stay and take care of you for a while and she left me here to keep an eye on you." She held up the portable phone. "She gave me this. I'm supposed to dial 911 if you need help. Do you need help?" she asked, leaning forward expectantly, her fingers poised over the numbers.

J.D. scowled. "No, I don't need help. I just need to go to the bathroom."

Marissa hopped down from the chair, carefully laid the phone on the seat, then bent down out of sight. When she straightened, she held a Mason jar in her hands. "Here," she said, holding it out to him. "Mama said you aren't supposed to get out of bed, no matter what. She said for you to make pee-pee in this jar."

J.D. looked from the jar to the face of the little girl who held it. Her eyes were the same shade of innocence as her mother's. Heat flooded his cheeks. He snatched the jar from her hands. "Now beat it," he grumped.

Marissa folded her arms stubbornly across her chest

and shook her head. "Can't. Mama said I'm not to leave you alone for even one second."

J.D. stifled a groan. If they didn't settle this pretty dang quick, whether or not Marissa was in the room would no longer be an issue. He couldn't hold it much longer. "How about if you step outside the door while I make pee-pee?" he asked reasonably. "When I'm done, I'll holler and you can come back in."

Marissa looked at him doubtfully for a moment, then shook her head again. "No way. If Mama came back and found out we'd disobeyed her, she'd skin both our hides."

J.D. stifled a groan. "Tell you what," he finally said, a pain threatening to match the one in his leg throbbing to life between his temples. "While I'm taking care of business here, you could trot over to the kitchen and fetch me one of those pain pills and a glass of water. Then you'd be taking care of me, just like your mother told you to, now wouldn't you?"

She continued to look at him, her mouth curved in a pouty frown. "And you won't get out of bed while I'm gone?"

J.D. held up two fingers. "Scout's honor."

"Well, all right," she said reluctantly. "But if you do, I'm telling Mama. Then you'll be sorry," she warned.

Chapter Three

Joanie sat in the chair Marissa had sat in earlier, her chin dipped to her chest, her arms folded beneath her breasts, her feet propped against the side of J.D.'s bed. At some point during the wee hours of the night, she must have drifted off because she awakened to sunshine warming her face. Stretching her arms above her head to loosen the kinks the night in the chair had placed in her back, she glanced toward J.D. He lay on his back not a foot away, his arm slung across his eyes, his chest rising and falling in the even rhythm of sleep.

She breathed a sigh of relief. The night had been a rough one, with him tossing and turning and moaning while she'd tried to keep him still and his leg elevated to keep it from swelling any more than it already was. She was glad to see that he rested peacefully now.

While she'd slept, he had managed to kick the bed

covers off his good leg, although the sheet still tented the leg encased in the cast. The white cloth dipped in soft gathers at his crotch and slanted across his groin, revealing an enticing expanse of bare, dark skin.

The sight reminded her of the feel of that same skin, heated in passion, rubbing against her own fevered flesh. Sensation swirled low in her abdomen as memories surfaced, and unconsciously she laid a hand there, remembering the seed planted the night they'd shared. She hadn't had time think about the baby since Doc Reynolds had confirmed her pregnancy the day before, not with J.D.'s unexpected arrival in Liberty Hill, then his accident.

A baby, she thought, still unable to believe it. J.D.'s baby.

She shifted her gaze to his face. Would the baby look like him? she wondered. Would he inherit his father's dark complexion, those irresistible blue eyes? A soft smile teased at one corner of her mouth as she touched a finger to the furrowed skin between his eyes and smoothed away the frown. Along with, of course, his stubbornness and his irreverent charm.

A soft sigh escaped her lips as she looked at him. She knew she had to tell him the news soon; delaying only made the telling more difficult. But what he would say when he learned he'd fathered a child? she wondered. What would he do? Would he think she'd lied when she had assured him she was protected? Would he be angry with her? Would he refuse to be a part of the child's life?

She'd never deluded herself into believing a marriage proposal would be forthcoming, nor did she want one. J.D. simply wasn't the marrying kind. The years he'd lived as a bachelor and the broken hearts he'd left in his wake were proof enough of that. But she hoped for the baby's sake that he would choose to share in its life.

Unable to resist touching him again, she lifted a lock of hair from his forehead and smoothed it back in place. His reaction wouldn't matter one way or the other, she told herself. She wouldn't let it. What was done was done, and if he refused to acknowledge the child, Joanie would just love it enough for them both.

Sighing wistfully, she started to turn away, then gasped when she was snagged at the waist and jerked back around. Before she knew what was happening, she was hauled across J.D.'s length.

Fisting her hands in the mattress on either side of his head, she pushed herself up until she could see his face. "J.D.!" she gasped. "What do you think you're doing?"

His eyes remained hooded, but a lusty smile curved one side of his mouth. He hiked one of her legs over his cast so that she straddled him, then he shifted to a more comfortable position beneath her. He closed his hands over her rear and snugged her against his groin. His sigh of satisfaction seared her cheek like a blowtorch.

"I'm about to claim me a kiss," he replied, his voice husky.

Wondering what in the world had come over him, Joanie tried to dodge him, but his hands caught the back of her head and held her in place while he lifted his own head to meet hers. He warmed her lips with his breath first, then moistened them with his tongue before closing his mouth over hers. Joanie knotted her fingers in the sheets as she fought the seductive pull of his kiss.

It's the drugs, she told herself, trying to distance herself from the sensations he was stirring. J.D. wouldn't be cozied up to her like this if he had his full wits about him. She'd seen the look on his face when he'd encountered all those kids at her house. If he hadn't fallen out of the tree and broken his leg, he'd probably still be running. She had to remember that, she told herself.

But then his tongue slipped between her parted lips, dipping deep into her mouth, sending rivers of warmth flooding through her middle, and her mind went blank. Her body turned traitor, responding to him in the most elemental of ways. She melted against him, her breasts flattening against his chest, her hips moving in a slow, undulating circle, chafing against him until his manhood swelled to life against her thigh.

Moaning his approval, he moved his hands to her waist, shifting her slightly until the swell she'd created rested in the soft curve of her pelvic bone. Satisfied, he slipped his hands beneath her shirt and skimmed them upward along her heated flesh until his fingertips grazed her breasts. Her nipples hardened in response to his gentle prodding and she arched away from him, unintentionally giving him easier access.

"Oh, baby," he murmured, "you feel so good."

"J.D.," she whispered helplessly, "you've got to stop. You don't know what you're doing."

"Sure I do," he said as he levered her body higher along his chest. "I'm making love to you." Pushing the plackets of her shirt aside with his nose, he exposed a breast, leaving a trail of fire along her skin with his tongue until he reached the already budded nipple. He closed his mouth over it, his tongue like coarse velvet against her tender flesh as he gently suckled.

A shiver rocked Joanie from her scalp to her toes. Whatever control she'd managed to hold on to was quickly slipping away. "J.D., please," she almost wept. "You've got to stop."

When he continued to ignore her, she clamped her hands on either side of his face, forcing his lips from her breast and his face to hers.

"J.D., look at me," she ordered, her voice shaking.

He smiled drunkenly and tried his best to conform to her request, forcing his lids open, then narrowing them against the glare of sunlight streaming through the bedroom window. He peered at her through the slits, his eyes unfocused and glazed.

Joanie glanced at the nightstand and saw the bottle of pain pills and the half-empty glass of water. How had they gotten there? She'd purposely left the bottle in the kitchen so she could monitor the number of pills he took. She glanced at him suspiciously. "J.D., did you take any pills other than the one I gave you?"

He frowned. "Pills?" he repeated. "Don't want any more pills," he argued, his words thick and slurred. "Want you." He twisted free of her hands and grabbed her shoulders, pulling her down, centering his mouth once again over the exposed nipple.

"Mama? Where are you?"

Joanie tensed at the sound of Marissa's voice, her fingers digging into J.D.'s flesh. He went still beneath her, his eyes opening wide to meet hers. She jerked her shirt back down into place. "Back here, Marissa," she called, trying to make her voice sound normal as she struggled to untangle herself from J.D.

She rolled to a standing position at the side of the bed just as Marissa burst through the door. Marissa headed straight for the bed, climbed up at its foot and crawled across its length. By the time she settled at the headboard beside J.D., he was sober as a judge.

He grabbed for the sheet and jerked it across his waist to hide his arousal. His eyes filled with panic, he tore his gaze from Marissa to stare at Joanie. "What are y'all still doing here?" he whispered hoarsely, looking at Joanie as if seeing her for the first time. "I told you to go home."

Joanie's cheeks still burned from the passion J.D. had stroked to life within her, but his bewildered look proved what she'd feared…he hadn't known who she was when he was making love to her. She bit back the disappointment that knowledge brought. "How much do you remember about last night?" she asked, evading his question.

His forehead plowed into a deep frown. His gaze slowly moved back to Marissa, as events slowly unfolded. "I remember waking up and finding her here," he said with a nod toward the little girl. "She told me you had gone home for a change of clothes and left her to look after me. She gave me another pill for the pain. I don't remember anything after that."

Marissa snuggled closer to J.D.'s chest. He shrank away as if a rattlesnake had coiled up alongside him.

Joanie swallowed a laugh at the look of sheer terror on his face. "She won't bite," she told him, her voice tinged with laughter.

J.D. whipped his head around to glare at her. "You

haven't answered my question yet," he said irritably. "Why are y'all still here?"

Joanie shrugged. "We couldn't very well leave you when you weren't able to take care of yourself."

His frown deepened into a scowl and he folded his arms across his chest. "I don't need taking care of. I've been doing a damn good job of just that all by myself for years."

Joanie arched a doubtful brow at his cast. "That may have been true in the past," she conceded with a nod. "But now you have a broken leg we are responsible for. Knowing that, if anything else happened to you, we wouldn't be able to forgive ourselves, would we, Marissa?" she asked, shifting her gaze to her daughter.

Marissa's expression turned somber as she looked from her mother to J.D. "Never," she replied emphatically. She laid a hand on his chest and patted softly, her lips puckering into a Shirley Temple pout. "I really am sorry you fell out of our tree and broke your leg. Does it hurt very much this morning?"

J.D. shifted uncomfortably. At the moment, something else was aching a lot more than his leg, but he couldn't very well tell the kid that. "No," he muttered. "Not too badly."

Joanie sensed his discomfort and suspected its cause. Though she wasn't sure J.D. deserved rescuing, she decided to give him a break. "Marissa, sweetheart, I bought some orange juice last night. It's in the refrigerator. Why don't you pour yourself and your brother a glass while I help J.D. get dressed?"

Though it was obvious the child would've preferred to stay right where she was, Marissa murmured obediently, "Okay, Mama." She gave J.D.'s chest one last pat, then dug her heels into the mattress and scooted off the bed.

J.D. waited until she was out of earshot. "And just exactly how long are you planning on staying?" he asked, eyeing Joanie suspiciously.

"Until you get your walking cast," she replied as she carefully shifted his leg from the pile of pillows.

J.D. jackknifed to a sitting position, his eyes widened in shock. "But that might be a whole week," he cried.

Joanie nodded and turned to carefully stack the pillows on the chair by the bed. "I know, but don't let that worry you," she assured him. "You'll never even know we're here."

You'll never even know we're here. J.D. snorted. That was worth a laugh…at least it would have been if he felt like laughing, which he didn't. He tossed the razor down and smoothed a hand over his cheek, frowning at his reflection in the bathroom mirror.

Cartoons blared from the television set in the den, pans rattled in the kitchen, the washing machine chugged away in the laundry room and above it all he could hear the constant squabbling of two five-year-olds. A man who'd lived his entire adult life alone, he found the noise was slowly driving him crazy.

And to think that less than twenty-four hours ago, he'd been looking forward to the possibility of spending another night with Joanie Summers. The very thought made him shudder in revulsion.

He had to get them out of his house, he told himself. But how? His chest rose and fell in a weary sigh.

Joanie would never leave. Not willingly. She was too
damn decent a human being. She felt responsible for
his breaking his leg. He'd just have to prove to her
that he could manage on his own, at least until he
could get a message to Manuel in Mexico and tell him
to hightail it back home.

He eyed the crutches propped against the wall by
the door. As much as he despised the damn things, he
knew he needed them. Until his cast was replaced with
a walking one, the crutches were his only hope of
mobility.

Grumbling under his breath, he snugged the
crutches under his arms and swung out the bathroom
door, wearing nothing more than his skivvies.

Joanie met him in the hall.

J.D. bit back a curse.

"Are you ready to get dressed?" she asked, wiping
her hands with a dishcloth.

"I can dress myself."

"I know, but since I'm here, why don't I help?"
She ducked through the bedroom door ahead of him
before he could stop her. She plucked a pair of jeans
from the bed and held them up for his inspection. "I
hope you don't mind, but I took the liberty of splitting
the seam on another pair of jeans while you were
freshening up. If I wash every day, maybe we'll only
have to ruin two pair." She gestured at the bed. "I
think it'd be easier if you sat down here and we eased
them up and over your cast."

J.D. wanted to argue with her...no, he wanted to
yell at her, to crack her over the head with the crutches
just to see if he could get her attention long enough
to convince her that he didn't need or want her help.

But he knew it was useless. She was going to help him dress whether he wanted her to or not.

He twisted around and sat, propping the crutches on the bed at his side. Joanie dropped to her knees in front of him, bending to hold the waist of his jeans open. His face burning in humiliation, J.D. lifted the broken leg and allowed Joanie to ease the jeans over his cast and up his leg. When she started to do the same for his good leg, he shoved her hands out of the way.

"I'm not totally helpless," he muttered as he stuffed his leg in and worked the waist of his jeans to his thighs. He stood, hopping on his good foot while he hitched them up over his hips, then turned his back to button his fly, clinging to that last thread of modesty.

It was such a masculine act and one Joanie hadn't witnessed in a while. Muscles bunched on his arms and across his back as he struggled to work the buttons through the holes. Her mouth watered at the sight. She swallowed quickly and looked away, reaching for his shirt. "I guess the first thing we'll need to do is clean the stalls and feed the stock, right?" she asked.

"Yeah, but I can handle it."

Joanie fisted her fingers in his shirt to keep from slugging him. As irresistible as he was, the man was as stubborn as a mule. "J.D., you can hardly make it to the bathroom by yourself. How in the world do you think you are going to throw hay and clean out stalls?"

"I'll figure out a way."

"Oh, for pity's sake!" She tossed the shirt at him. "We'll be in the truck."

J.D. ducked, managing to catch the shirt before it slapped him in the face. He sank back on the edge of the bed as he watched Joanie march from the room, her back as straight as a poker.

We'll be in the truck? Is that what she'd said? A shiver worked its way down his spine, because he feared he knew who "we" was. She was planning on the kids going along.

He buried his face in the shirt, groaning his frustration, knowing full well that if he wasn't a grown man, more than likely he'd bawl like a baby.

The bossy streak J.D. had first discovered in Joanie at the emergency room and grown to detest in the short time she'd taken up residence in his house came into play full force once they reached the barns.

With strict orders for him to remain in the truck, she perched her kids on the fence, then rolled two of the fifty-gallon barrels he used to train horses for barrel racing into the holding pen and laid them on their sides.

"What in the hell is she doing?" he mumbled under his breath as he watched her disappear into the tack room. His curiosity got the better of him and he climbed from the truck, snagged his crutches and hobbled over to the fence in time to see Joanie reappear, dragging two saddles through the dirt behind her. After strapping the saddles onto the barrels, she motioned for the kids to climb down from the fence and join her.

J.D. started to chuckle when he realized her intent.

"Okay, guys," she said as she plopped first one twin, then the other onto the saddled barrels. "Ride as long as you please. If you need me, I'll be in the barn with J.D. cleaning out the stalls.''

"Pretty creative," he murmured in approval as Joanie stepped through the gate, then turned to lock it behind her.

"Mothers have to be," she replied. Wiping her hands on the seat of her jeans, she turned to him. "I saw a front-end loader parked at the far end of the barn. Is that what you use to haul the muck from the stalls?"

"Yeah."

She heaved a deep breath, then turned and headed for the barn. "You drive. I'll shovel," she called over her shoulder.

"Now wait a minute," J.D. argued and swung the crutches into motion to catch up. "I can't ask you—"

Joanie whirled so fast J.D. had to rock back on his crutches to keep from mowing her down. "You didn't ask. I offered. Now where do you keep your shovels?"

Since all that was required to operate the front-end loader were two good hands and a foot, it made sense for J.D. to be the one to operate the machine...but it grieved his manly spirit to have a woman doing the manual labor while he sat on his butt pushing levers. Just the same, he gave in, knowing she was right. "They're hanging on pegs by the north door," he replied sullenly.

To compound his guilt, he soon discovered it didn't take him nearly as long to drive from the barn to the manure pile out back as it did Joanie to shovel out stalls. As a result, he spent a lot of his time sitting and watching while she worked.

For a woman, he had to admit, she handled a shovel

like a pro. Dressed in jeans and boots, the tails of her sleeveless shirt knotted at her waist, she moved like a whirlwind from stall to stall, filling the bucket on the front-end loader, then spreading fresh straw in the stalls.

Though watching her work so hard made him feel lower than dirt, looking at her was certainly no hardship. With each dip and thrust of the shovel, the muscles in her bottom tightened, drawing his eye there. He didn't have to stretch far to imagine the feel of those muscles, bare beneath his hands. He'd experienced the pleasure firsthand only hours before and more thoroughly a couple months back. The memories of that night of loving in San Antonio surfaced, haunting him with the pleasures they'd shared. It was all he could do to stay on the front-end loader and not hop down and pin her against the wall of the stall and sink his fingers into that sweet flesh again.

Sounds of the kids whooping and hollering from the holding pen drifted through the barn's open doors and J.D. gave himself a hard shake, tearing his gaze away from Joanie's backside. It wouldn't do to let himself consider for even a minute a relationship with her. She was a mother twice over, and though J.D. had played with the idea of striking up a relationship with Joanie over the weeks since he'd bedded her in San Antonio, he sure as hell wasn't interested in taking on any kids.

One of seven himself, he knew what a responsibility kids were and what a drain on the pocketbook they could be. Hadn't he heard his old man complain of that often enough over the years to know? That was one of the reasons he'd remained single for so long, choosing instead to spend his time and money establishing a first-class quarter-horse farm rather than start-ing a family. He'd watched his father's frustrations as he'd struggled to make ends meet while his dreams of being a number-one horse breeder remained just out of reach.

Though J.D. didn't share much with his father, he did share his old man's dream of owning a top-notch quarter-horse farm, and he refused to make the same choices—or mistakes, depending upon how a man chose to look at them—as his father had made. He'd made his sacrifices, riding the rodeo circuit for years, for the most part living out of his truck while he stashed his prize money in the bank, saving for the day he could buy his own place. Sixteen years and several broken bones later, he finally had his dream.

Now, same as then, his number-one priority was his farm. He wouldn't lose sight of that dream because of some pretty little woman with an enticing backside.

Especially one with kids.

Marissa lay on her stomach on a hay bale opposite the one J.D. sat on, her chin propped in her hands and her feet kicked up in the air, watching while he soaped halters.

"What are those initials on the back of your belt for?" she asked.

J.D. jabbed his rag into the can of saddle soap, then slapped it against the strip of leather and rubbed, his ears ringing from the constant flow of questions shot at him. Before he could respond to this one, Shane chimed in, saving him the bother.

"It's his name, silly," he called from above them,

where he walked the top plank of the stall as if it was a tightrope.

Marissa clapped a hand over her mouth and giggled. "What's the matter?" she asked in a sassy voice. "Afraid you'll forget your own name?"

J.D. glanced up at her from beneath his brows and scowled, inwardly praying that Joanie would return soon from her trip into town and save him from these two before he went stark raving mad.

Shane jumped to the ground, then stood, dusting loose straw from his jeans. "No, stupid. All cowboys wear their names on their belts, don't they, J.D.?"

J.D. pretended disinterest, hoping they'd leave him out of their conversation. "I suppose," he mumbled.

"Well, you don't have a belt with your name on it, Mr. Smarty Pants," Marissa taunted her brother. "So you must not be a cowboy."

J.D. watched out of the corner of his eye as Shane ducked his head and kicked at the loose straw on the barn floor and knew how badly the comment hurt the boy. With four sisters of his own, he'd learned from experience what a pain in the butt a smart-mouthed little sister could be. Knowing this, he tossed the rag aside and leaned over to hang the bridle on the hook. "He just hasn't earned his yet," J.D. said, coming to Shane's defense. "He'll get his one day."

Marissa looked at him suspiciously. "How?"

J.D. shrugged as he screwed the lid back on the can of saddle soap, stalling while he tried to think up a good explanation. "There's no one particular way," he said, making the story up as he went. "You just have to prove your worth as a cowboy. My daddy gave me my first one after I saddle broke my first horse."

Marissa sat up, wrapping her arms around her legs and tucking her knees under her chin. "Shane won't get one that way 'cause we don't have a daddy."

Shane spun to glare at his sister.

"Well, it's true," she said defensively. "We *don't* have a daddy." With a haughty lift of her chin, she turned her attention back to J.D. "He ran off and left us when we were just babies," she explained for his benefit. "He comes to see us every once in a while, but mama says it doesn't matter 'cause she's got enough love in her heart for both a mama and daddy put together."

J.D. wasn't sure he wanted to hear any of this, but it didn't appear he had much choice as Marissa seemed bound and determined to spill her guts right there on the barn floor.

"Mimi, that's my daddy's mama, keeps hoping that he'll come back and live with us again and be our daddy. Pawpaw says it'll never happen, that my daddy doesn't have a responsible bone in his body." Her forehead pulled into a frown as a new thought formed. "Do you suppose he broke it, like you did your leg?"

"Broke what?" J.D. asked, having a tough time keeping up with her train of thought.

"His responsible bone."

J.D. sputtered a laugh, then quickly sobered when he saw the earnestness in Marissa's expression. "No, sugar," he said kindly. "There's no such thing as a responsible bone. That's just an expression."

"Oh," she said, her shoulders sagging. "I was hoping that maybe if we put it in a cast like the doctor did your leg, we could fix his responsible bone and maybe he'd come back."

"We don't want him back," Shane mumbled, surprising J.D. with the amount of anger in his voice.

"Do, too," Marissa argued.

A shadow fell across the tack-room floor. All three glanced up to see Joanie standing in the doorway. J.D. felt a pang of guilt at the sight of her. She looked tired. Dead tired. Her eyes were shadowed with dark circles, a sign, he was sure, of the sleep she'd lost the night before while looking after him.

"What are you two fussing about now?" she asked, fisting her hands on her hips.

Suspecting that she might not like the idea of her kids sharing the intimacies of her private life with him, J.D. leaned over to ruffle Marissa's hair, praying the kids would follow his lead. "Marissa here seems to think that I have to wear this tooled belt with my initials carved in it so I won't forget my name. Isn't that right, Marissa?"

The child turned her gaze on J.D., her eyes bright, obviously enjoying the attention turned her way. "Yeah," she agreed, then grinned, her eyes sparking with mischief. "What does J.D. stand for anyway?"

J.D. sent up a silent prayer of thanks that he'd succeeded in diverting the conversation to a less intrusive one. "Well, nothing," he said. "That's just my name."

Obviously, Marissa didn't buy his explanation because she turned to her mother for verification. "Do you know what it stands for, Mama?"

Joanie shrugged, unable to remember J.D. being called anything other than that—J.D. "I don't know, probably something awful like John Delbert."

"John Delbert!" the twins echoed, laughing.

"Before you bust a gut laughing so hard," J.D. replied dryly, "John Delbert is not my name."

"Well, what is it, then?" Marissa asked.

"J.D. Plain and simple." When they continued to look at him as if they didn't believe him, he threw up his hands. "Can I help it if my mother didn't have much of an imagination?"

Joanie just shook her head, chuckling. "Okay, you two," she ordered, waving the kids toward the door. "Time to head for the house."

"Do we have to?" Marissa whined.

Joanie dipped her chin, giving her children one of those mother looks J.D. remembered his own mother owning. "You certainly do. It's time to get baths, eat your dinner and hit the sack."

"But we're not tired," the twins chimed in harmony.

J.D. watched Joanie's shoulders droop and remembered the hours she'd spent mucking out the stalls and feeding. Backbreaking work even if a person was used to it. He struggled to his feet, swaying slightly after sitting for so long. "Boy, *I* sure am," he said, hoping to save Joanie a battle she obviously didn't have the energy for. "Marissa, honey, would you hand me my crutches? And, Shane, would you mind putting that can of saddle soap back on the shelf, son?"

Both kids hustled to do his bidding, then fell in beside him, chattering like magpies as they vied for his attention while they escorted him out to the truck.

Joanie stood in the tack room, staring after them, her jaw slack, wondering what spell J.D. had cast over her children.

Or better yet, what spell her children had cast over J.D.

J.D. sat in his recliner, frowning at the television while Joanie sat perched on the sofa, her feet tucked beneath her, smelling like a damn rose garden. He sniffed and folded his arms across his chest, trying to pretend he didn't notice. But, hell, how could he keep from noticing her?

Fresh from a shower, her cheeks scrubbed to a healthy glow, she wore nothing but a light cotton robe, a feminine thing covered in tiny pink rosebuds with a shawl-like collar that veed at her breast. A belt at the waist kept its panels modestly in place...until it reached her knees. There it gaped, revealing the feminine curve of her leg and just enough bare thigh to whet a man's curiosity.

Careful not to let on that he was watching her, he studied her out of the corner of his eye. She sat with his jeans gathered in her lap while she nimbly threaded the strip of leather through the holes she'd punched in the split leg of his jeans. Light from a floor lamp beside the sofa panned the gold from her hair while offering her enough light to see the almost invisible holes. She kept her head tilted at a slight angle to keep from throwing a shadow on her work.

He couldn't help wondering if the woman ever sat still. She and her kids had been in his house for three days, three lo-o-ng days, and he still hadn't figured out when she found time to rest.

When he awoke each morning, she was already in the kitchen cooking breakfast and usually had a load of laundry chugging away in the washing machine. At the barns she worked right alongside him, cleaning stalls, feeding the stock, and even helped hook the horses up to the walker for their daily exercise while still managing to throw something together for a midday meal.

After lunch she always succeeded in browbeating J.D. into elevating his leg to cut down on the swelling while the kids took their afternoon nap. Instead of putting up her own feet and taking advantage of the quiet, Joanie started dinner.

A lock of hair refused to stay in place and kept slipping from behind her ear to spill across her cheek. He watched in growing fascination while she paused again and again in her work to twist it behind her ear.

Drawn by the movement, he stared, mesmerized by the delicate pink shell of her ear. Turning slightly, he let his gaze slip down the slender column of her neck to the spot on her cotton robe right at breast level, where the fabric moved with each rhythmic beat of her heart. Budded to a tight knot of temptation, her nipple pushed against the thin fabric. He felt a tightening in his jeans and jerked his gaze away with a muffled curse.

Joanie glanced up. "Did you say something, J.D.?" He grunted an unintelligible answer that Joanie took for a no. A soft smile curved at her mouth. "You're not accustomed to having people around all the time, are you?"

He kept his eyes glued to the television screen, pretending interest in the news. "No."

She chuckled. "From a man who grew up with six brothers and sisters, I find that hard to believe."

"Yeah, but that was a long time ago. For the past sixteen years, I've lived alone."

Joanie poked the leather strip into a hole, then slowly pulled it through. "Why did you never marry?"

"I am married." He let a heart-stopping second pass before he added, "To my farm."

Joanie let her breath ease out. "An odd choice in a mate."

"It suits me."

Joanie smiled again. "Yes, it does." She threaded the leather strip through another hole. "But still, I'd think that a man who loves women as much as you do would have taken a wife by now."

"Can't have both."

Surprised by the comment, Joanie let her hands and her work drop to her lap. "Why not?"

He scrunched down in his chair, not liking the direction the conversation was taking. "Takes a lot of money and time to build a first-class breeding farm and that's exactly what I intend to own—a first-class facility. A wife and kids would only hold me back."

Joanie could only stare, surprised by the almost venom-like tone of his voice. She remembered her ex-husband spouting almost those same words, but instead of a horse farm, he'd just wanted the freedom to pursue a good time. "And how would you know a family would hold you back since you've never had one?"

His mouth curled in a scowl as he continued to frown at the television screen. "I don't have to have one to know. I was part of one that kept my father from realizing his dreams. Nobody is going to stand between me and mine."

Chapter Four

If Joanie had needed confirmation that a marriage proposal wouldn't be forthcoming when she finally found the courage to tell J.D. about the baby, his comment certainly offered it. It also put a hiatus on her plan to tell him about her pregnancy that night.

She stuffed the leather through the last hole, then glanced his way. He still sat in his recliner, scowling at the television set.

She swallowed hard. *I'll tell him when he takes us home,* she promised herself. It was a cowardly act, she knew, but she didn't relish the idea of having to be around him for any length of time once he knew he was about to become a father.

"Are you sure you don't want me to go back and get those crutches?"

J.D. heaved a weary sigh, but kept his eyes set on the end of the corridor and the door that led outside, anxious to get out of the hospital. "No, Joanie, I don't. That's why they call it a walking cast. You walk on it."

"I know, but it just seems so soon to be putting weight on that leg."

"For crying out loud, it's been a week!"

"A week isn't that—"

"Joanie!" a voice called.

Joanie glanced up to see Doc Reynolds making his way around the corner of the nurses' station and heading her way. Her pulse skittered into a nervous rhythm at the sight of him, and she was tempted to run, but she stopped, forcing a smile as she waited for him to reach her. "Hi, Doc."

"What are you doing here at the hospital? You're not having any problems, are you?"

Joanie shook her head. "Oh, no. I just drove J.D. over to get his cast changed."

Doc stepped closer, lifting his chin to study her through his bifocals while he buried his hands in the pockets of his white jacket. "You're looking a little peaked. Are you getting enough rest?"

Out of the corner of her eye, Joanie saw the curious look J.D. sent her way and knew she had to get him away before Doc inadvertently revealed her condition. "Every chance I get!" she said and forced a bright smile.

"Are you taking those vitamins I prescribed?"

"Yes, sir, I sure am." She caught J.D. by the arm. "You'll have to excuse us, Doc, but we've got to scoot. The kids are at Mother's Day Out, and if I'm late, they charge me double.'' She all but dragged J.D. down the hall, leaving Doc Reynolds standing in the hallway, staring after her.

Once they'd passed through the hospital entrance, J.D. shook free. ''Damn, Joanie. It's a walking cast, not a jogging one.''

''Oh, sorry.'' Her hand shaking, she dug in her pocket for the keys and tossed them to J.D. ''You drive,'' she said and headed for the truck at a fast trot.

''Well, thanks,'' he murmured dryly, frowning at her bossy back. ''Don't mind if I do.''

Once in the truck and headed for home, Joanie relaxed a little…but not much. The encounter with Doc Reynolds had been a close one and reminded her of the task that still lay ahead. She'd put it off as long as she could.

They drove in silence until they reached the city limits of Liberty Hill. Trying to think how best to break the news to him, Joanie sat beside J.D., her knee bouncing ninety-to-nothing, her fingers tapping nervously against her thighs.

J.D. cut a surreptitious glance her way, noticing her nervous movements, and suddenly remembered the doctor's odd comments. ''You're not sick or anything, are you?'' he asked curiously.

Joanie whipped her head around to look at him. ''Me? Heck no.''

''What did that old man back there mean, then, when he asked if you were getting enough rest and taking your vitamins?''

''Doc Reynolds?'' At his nod, she turned her face to peer out the windshield, so he couldn't see the lie in her eyes. ''Oh, he's an old worrywart. He's our family doctor and has been for years and is convinced I still need a nap and a dose of daily vitamins just like the twins." Hoping to distract him, she strained to look ahead. "Do you remember how to get to my house?"

"Yeah, but I thought you wanted to pick up the kids first?"

She glanced at her watch. "I do, but I know you're anxious to get back to the farm. We've got time to run by the house first and let me get my car."

J.D. made the turn onto her street and pulled up in front of her house. He killed the engine, then twisted around in his seat to look at Joanie, still wondering about her odd behavior. She looked healthy enough, but her explanation of the doctor's comments was unconvincing and he couldn't help wondering if she did suffer some ailment. Hard to believe, considering the pace she'd kept for the past week...which reminded him of all the long hours and the backbreaking work she'd done for him while she'd been at his farm. A stab of guilt pierced him at the thought.

"Listen, Joanie," he began slowly, "I know I probably didn't seem to appreciate all you did for me this past week, but, well...I do. It's just that I'm not used to having to depend on anyone other than myself and I'm sure as hell not accustomed to someone waiting on me hand and foot all the time."

Joanie saw how much the admission cost him and smiled ruefully. "I know you appreciated our help, J.D." She laid a hand on his arm, then just as quickly pulled the hand back to squeeze it between her knees. "Listen, J.D.," she began, then stopped, biting her lip when she felt unexpected tears spring to her eyes. She glanced away, cleared her throat and tried again. "I need to tell you something, but I don't quite know how to say it."

A frown knitted his brow. "What?"

She turned to look at him. "Well..." She hesitated a moment longer, then decided there was no easy way to share the news. "I'm pregnant," she said, then braced herself for the explosion she knew was sure to follow.

He stared at her, his forehead plowing into deep furrows, then his eyes widened as what she'd just said slowly soaked in. His mouth opened, then closed. "You're—you're what?" he finally managed to choke out.

"Pregnant," she said again.

The blood slowly drained from his face. "And it's mine?"

"Yes."

He stared at her a long, heart-stopping moment before his jaw slowly tightened and a muscle began to tick there. "But you said—"

"I know," she cut in, hoping to forestall the anger she could see building. "And I am taking birth control pills. Or at least I was," she corrected, frowning. "For some reason, they don't work for me. Doc Reynolds said that happens sometimes."

"The man you spoke to at the hospital," he murmured at the mention of Doc Reynolds's name.

"Yes, he's my doctor."

He twisted back around in his seat and closed his hands over the steering wheel, his fingers curling tightly against its hardness. He stared through the windshield, his face a stiff, unreadable mask.

Joanie swallowed hard. "Please don't think I expect anything from you, J.D. I don't. I just felt that you should know you'd fathered a child." She reached out her hand and opened the door. "I'm sorry, J.D.," she murmured. "Really I am." Without waiting for a reply, she jumped down, slamming the door behind her and taking off for the house at a run.

Joanie stood at the kitchen window, the knuckle of her index finger caught between her teeth, while she watched J.D. sitting in his truck. He hadn't moved so much as a muscle since she'd left him more than five minutes before. He continued to sit behind the wheel, staring out the windshield, his fingers closed around the steering wheel.

She understood his shock, felt terrible that she was the cause of it, but was convinced she'd done the right thing in telling him about her pregnancy. He had a right to know he'd fathered a child. In time, she hoped he understood her reasons in sharing that information with him.

She wished that there had been a better way to break the news, a gentler method of making him aware, but in the end the simplest words were the only ones she could form. *I'm pregnant.* Innocent in their simplicity, but damning in delivery. A part of her cried out to him in understanding, because her own reaction hadn't been much different. Another part of her wept at the anger and the shock the news had drawn.

While she watched, he seemed to shake himself, then lowered a hand to the key in the ignition. The truck's engine sparked to life. Slowly, he pulled away from the curb, never once looking back.

Joanie felt her heart sink, knowing that she'd never see J. D. Cawthon again.

J.D. slipped the harness off the mare's head, stepped back and slapped her on the rump, signaling her that she was free. She tossed her head, nickering softly, then raced out into the pasture to join the other mares grazing there. Slipping the halter over his shoulder, J.D. pulled the gate shut behind him and wrapped the chain once around the brace, clipping it into place.

Pregnant.

He shook his head but was unable to shake free of the word that had haunted his every step for over a week. Hooking a boot over the bottom rail, he rested his forearms against the gate and stared off across the pasture, playing back the scene in his mind. Sitting in his truck with Joanie, watching while she fidgeted nervously before she'd laid the bomb on him.

After she'd jumped out of the truck and run into her house, he'd sat in front of her house a good five minutes, immobilized by shock.

Then anger had set in.

A careful man, he always made sure that he used protection when having sex with a woman. That night with Joanie in San Antonio hadn't been any different. He'd had a condom right there in his wallet. But when he'd reached for the wallet and the condom inside, she had told him it wasn't necessary, that she was protected. Like a fool, he'd taken her at her word.

Cursing, he slapped his open hand against the gate so hard the metal sang, stinging his hand. It was her fault, he told himself. She was the one who'd made the mistake, not him. She'd refused his offer of protection, so she could damn well live with the consequences.

And judging by what she'd said, she was prepared to do just that. It wasn't as if she expected anything from him. By her own admission, the only reason she'd told him that he had fathered a baby was that she'd thought it was his right to know.

Okay, so now he knew. End of story.

Groaning, he pressed his forehead against the iron rail. Then why couldn't he shut this episode out of his mind? Why couldn't he outrun the guilt that shadowed his every step? Why did the vision of Joanie sitting in his truck, huddled against the door, haunt him day and night?

She'd *told* him she didn't expect anything from him, he reminded himself. For most men, that was all the out they would have needed.

But J.D. was having a hard time accepting that out. Instead, he kept thinking of this young woman, divorced, already raising two children on her own, who was now carrying his child.

His child.

The very thought made a shiver run the length of his spine. No, he couldn't turn his back on her. As much as he wanted to, he couldn't do that.

He'd do the right thing by her, he told himself…just as soon as he figured out what the right thing was.

J.D. stood on the front porch of Joanie's house, his hat in his hand, his forehead and upper lip beaded in sweat, unable to find the strength—or the courage—to lift his hand to knock at the door. He dragged a bandanna from his back pocket and mopped at his face, wishing he could blame his discomfort on the heat.

He couldn't.

The sun had set more than an hour before and a night breeze cooled the air. The truth was, he was scared. More scared than he'd ever been in his entire life. A man who had climbed on some of the rankest stock horses the rodeo circuit had to offer, who had been bucked off, stomped on, dragged through the dirt by fifteen-hundred-pound horses, and then climbed right back on to do it all again, suddenly discovered that a yellow streak ran down the middle of his back.

Sighing, he stuffed the bandanna into his pocket and lifted his hand. This wasn't going to get any easier, he told himself. He might as well get it over with.

He knocked softly, not wanting to wake the kids. He'd purposely waited until he knew Joanie would have them in bed, wanting to talk to her alone. After a moment, the porch light clicked on and he ducked his head, squinting against the unexpected glare. The front door opened and he glanced up to see Joanie standing on the opposite side of the screen, her mouth slightly agape.

"J.D.?" she asked as if she couldn't believe it was him. "What are you doing here?"

"I need to talk to you," he mumbled, nervously working the brim of his hat through his fingers.

She flipped up the latch on the screen door, then pushed against its wooden frame, holding it open. "Come on in."

He hobbled past her, catching the scent of roses from her, the same scent that still hung in his house as a reminder that she'd been there. Once inside, he turned, waiting while she shut the door.

She crossed to him, gesturing for him to take a seat on the sofa. "Can I get you something to drink?" she asked politely.

Though a stiff shot of whiskey held a certain appeal, J.D. shook his head. "No, thank you." He dropped down on the sofa, stretching his cast out in front of him and hooking his hat on his good knee.

Joanie took a seat in a chair opposite him. "How's your leg?" she asked.

"Fine. I can pretty much do anything I want now." The silence seemed to stretch for endless seconds. "How are the kids?" he finally asked, stalling for time.

Joanie chuckled. "Driving me crazy. They're still talking about all the fun they had out at your place. Now they want me to buy them a horse."

J.D. couldn't help smiling himself. "Never met a kid yet that didn't dream of owning his own horse." He turned his gaze on his hat, studying it a moment, then twisted his mouth to one side and glanced back up at her. "You feeling okay?"

The question caught Joanie off guard. "Well, y-yes."

He let his gaze drop to her stomach and nodded his head in that direction. "How about—well, you know, the kid? How's it doing?"

Joanie tried not to laugh at his obvious discomfort. "'It' is doing just fine. Thanks for asking."

J.D. heaved a sigh. "I've been giving a lot of thought to this situation," he said after a moment. "And I want to apologize for putting all the blame on you. The fault's as much mine as yours. We made a mistake and I want you to know that I'm willing to do my part to make things right."

Butterflies took flight in Joanie's stomach. "What do you mean, 'make things right'?"

"Well, marry you, of course," he said, looking at her in surprise. "We can get our blood tests tomorrow, then find us a justice of the peace to do it all up legal."

Stunned, Joanie could only stare. She had never expected a marriage proposal. Not from J.D., the world contender for bachelor of the year. Ten years ago, she'd have leaped at the offer. Even now, as a mature woman and without the blinders of infatuation shading her reason, she might have considered his offer. Oh, who was she fooling? She'd have jumped at the chance to marry J.D. if love had been involved. But not now, not when the word 'love' had never passed between them and not when the proposal was offered out of a sense of obligation.

Needing the distraction that movement offered, she rose, shaking her head. "No," she murmured as she paced away. "I won't marry you."

"But, Joanie—" he began.

"No," she repeated more firmly, spinning to face him. "And nothing you say will change my mind."

"But why not?"

"J.D.," she said on a sigh, "I appreciate your offer. Really I do. But I won't marry you. I can't. You don't want the responsibility of a wife and children. You told me so yourself."

His mouth curled in a scowl at hearing his own words thrown back at him. "I wouldn't have offered to marry you if I wasn't willing to accept the responsibilities of taking on you and your brood."

Hearing her children referred to as a "brood" didn't offend Joanie, not when it came from J.D. In fact, hearing him acknowledge them at all and knowing that he was dead serious in offering to take them all on moved her incredibly. She stopped in front of him and stooped to gather his hands between hers.

"I know that you would, J.D.," she said softly. She sighed, easing back down in the chair opposite him, keeping his hands in hers. "But how long would it be before you grew to resent us?" She shook her head when he opened his mouth to argue the point. "I was married to a man who didn't want the responsibilities of a family. He left us when the twins weren't quite two. I won't put my children or myself through that emotional strain again."

J.D. frowned, remembering the conversation between Marissa and Shane when they'd aired their feelings about their father. To him, the man sounded like a good-for-nothing jerk and he wasn't at all sure he liked being put in the same category as Joanie's ex.

"Besides, marriage isn't necessary," she added. She squeezed his hands between hers. "Although I do appreciate your offering. It means a lot to know that the father of the child I carry is an honorable man."

J.D. felt heat flood his cheeks. At the moment, he didn't feel very honorable. He was too busy feeling relief that she'd turned down his offer. "But I have to do something," he argued. "I can't leave you to handle this all on your own."

"If you want to contribute financially to the baby's support, fine, J.D., do so. And if you choose to acknowledge the child and share in its life, that's fine, too. I'm sure we can work out some kind of arrangement that suits us both. But you can do all of that without marrying me. Whatever obligation you feel is to the baby, not to me."

"What about that cowboy you met up with in San Antonio?" Serena suggested. "Why don't you invite him to come down for the Labor Day celebration?"

Joanie tried to keep her face free of emotion at the mention of J.D. "Give it up, Serena. I'm not bringing a date. I'm bringing my children and that's final."

Serena flopped down in the beanbag chair in the twins' bedroom, pouting while she watched her friend fling shoes and a wild assortment of junk from the closet floor. "You're doomed to a single life, you know that, don't you?" she said petulantly.

Her head buried in the depths of the closet, Joanie replied in a muffled voice, "There's nothing wrong with being single, Serena. Just because you are dead set on keeping a man at your side, doesn't mean that every other woman of your acquaintance is required to do the same." She backed out of the closet with an armload of clothes. Puffing, she crossed to the bed and heaved them on top of the bedspread.

Serena rolled her eyes. "Why in God's name are you cleaning out the kids' closet? Don't most people do that in the spring?"

"Yes," Joanie replied, fighting for patience. "But school starts next week and I won't have time then." And when spring came, she'd have a new baby to care for, she added mentally. But she couldn't tell Serena that.

She straightened, putting a hand to the middle of her back to ease the ache. Already she was beginning to feel the burden of the baby she carried...and the secret she carried along with it. She hadn't told anyone but J.D. about her pregnancy, not even Serena, her best friend.

Serena leaned forward, straining to peer around Joanie. "Are you gaining weight?" she asked, frowning.

Joanie tugged the oversize shirt she wore to disguise her growing roundness back over her hips. "Probably. You know how it is, though," she said with a shrug. "With the kids out of school for the summer, we live on junk food."

Serena cocked her head, eyeing Joanie suspiciously. "Joanie Summers, you've never weighed an ounce over a hundred and ten in your life. Other than when you were pregnant with the twins, of course," she added.

At the word "pregnant," Joanie felt heat flood her cheeks. Never one who lied well, she quickly turned away to hide her guilt. Serena caught her by the hand before she could disappear into the closet again.

Joanie stopped but refused to turn around. "Hey," Serena said softly, "I didn't mean to hurt your feelings."

Tears sprang to Joanie's eyes and she silently cursed the roller coaster of emotions that was keeping her tied in knots.

When her friend didn't respond, Serena stood, still hanging on to Joanie's hand. She stepped in front of her, dipped her knees, then put a finger beneath Joanie's chin and tipped it up. At the sight of the tell-tale tears, she sucked in a sharp breath. She marched Joanie right to the bed and made her sit down. "What's the matter, Joanie?" she demanded as she sat down beside her. "And don't tell me it's none of my business. You know you can talk to me."

Joanie sighed, blinking back the tears, knowing that she could trust Serena with her secret but still reluctant to burden her friend with the news of her pregnancy. "It's nothing, really," she assured her friend, forcing a smile.

"Like hell it's nothing," Serena insisted. "You never cry. Now you tell me right this minute what has you so upset. I swear I'm not leaving until you do," she added stubbornly.

Joanie sighed again, her shoulders drooping under the weight of the burden she'd carried alone for almost two full months. "You have to swear to me you won't tell anyone," she said.

Serena held up her hand. "I swear."

Taking a deep breath, Joanie murmured, "I'm pregnant," then scrunched her shoulders to her ears, waiting for Serena to explode. When nothing happened, she glanced over at her friend to see her staring at her, her eyes bulging open and her mouth gaping wide.

"Pregnant," Serena finally said, the single word coming out on a disbelieving breath. "But who? When?"

Joanie picked up one of Marissa's T-shirts from the bed and carefully folded it. "J. D. Cawthon. That weekend you and I were in San Antonio."

Serena let out a low whistle as she slowly absorbed the news. "Have you told him?"

"Yes."

"And?" Serena prompted.

"And...nothing." Joanie rose quickly and crossed to the dresser, hoping she could escape any more questions. She opened a drawer and tucked in the folded shirt, then pushed the drawer shut with her knee.

"What do you mean, nothing?" Serena demanded, rising to follow Joanie. "The guy has a responsibility here."

"I know that."

"So tell him he has to marry you!"

"He offered."

"And you refused," Serena finished for her. She slapped a hand to her forehead. "Jeez, Joanie. What are you thinking? You're already raising two children on your own and barely making ends meet. How will you manage with three?"

"J.D. will help out financially when he can."

Serena tossed up a hand. "Oh, great! So he'll throw a little money your way when it's convenient for him to do so." She fisted her hands on her hips. "What happens to you and the kids during the times when he can't?"

"I'll manage."

"You'll manage on a teacher's salary?" Serena tossed back her head and laughed. "And pigs fly!" She paced the length of the room, pushing her bangs from her forehead. "What about your job? Have you told anyone at the school yet?"

"No! And please," Joanie begged, "promise me that you won't tell anyone, either."

Serena just shook her head as if disgusted that Joanie would think it necessary to ask such a thing.

"I won't tell anyone, Joanie, but how long do you think you can hide your pregnancy?"

"I hope that I can teach for another two months before I offer my resignation."

"Resignation!" the other woman echoed. "If you resign, how will you support yourself and the kids? Joanie, you're not thinking this through!"

"Yes, I am. I'll have my disability income and I can withdraw my teacher's retirement, plus I have a little savings set aside in the bank."

Serena flopped back down on the beanbag and buried her face in her hands. "Joanie, Joanie, Joanie," she wailed. "Call the guy. Tell him you've changed your mind, that you want to marry him. If not for yourself, think of the kids."

Joanie crossed to Serena and placed a hand on her friend's shoulder. "I am thinking of the kids, Serena. I won't make them suffer through another divorce."

Serena jerked her head up. "Who said anything about divorce? We're talking marriage here, not divorce!"

Joanie dropped down to her knees beside the beanbag chair, determined to make Serena understand. "But what happens when J.D. decides that he's bitten off a little more than he's willing to chew? He'll leave, just like their daddy did. I won't put Marissa and Shane through that again. I can't."

Joanie climbed from her car and stood, stretching the kinks out of her back. The day at the lake for Serena's annual Labor Day picnic had taken its toll. "Okay, kids," she said, her voice heavy with weariness, "Let's get the car unloaded. Shane, you grab the cooler. Marissa, you bring the beach bag and the wet towels.'' She popped the lid on the trunk and waited while the kids followed her instructions, unaffected by their grumbling.

Once they were out of the way, she looped an arm through the picnic basket with a weary sigh, then stepped back to lower the trunk lid.

A thud and a squeal behind her had her wheeling and she nearly tripped over the cooler and beach bag that had been dumped on the driveway behind her.

''J.D.!'' the twins screamed, already racing down the driveway to meet the truck pulling up at the curb.

J.D. climbed down from the cab, then fought to keep his balance as the twins slammed into him, each wrapping their arms around a leg and hanging on. ''Well, hi,'' he said, totally taken back by the greeting. ''What have you kids been up to?''

Marissa kept her arms wrapped around his thigh and leaned back to grin up at him. ''We've been to the lake.''

''Yeah, we went tubing and had a picnic,'' Shane added.

''Tubing, huh?'' J.D. reached down and ruffled Shane's hair, then scooped Marissa up in his arms before she made them both take a fall.

''Yeah, but Mama wouldn't ride on the tube,'' Marissa added, scrunching her nose. ''She said she's getting too old for such nonsense.''

J.D. shifted his gaze to see Joanie walking down the drive to meet them. *Too old?* Not to his way of thinking.

The Empire-style sundress she wore buttoned down the front to end at midcalf. The last four buttons were undone and with each step the skirt fluttered open, revealing bare, tanned legs. His heart did a little flop at the sight, but he told himself the sensation was just gas from the barbecue sandwich he'd choked down on the way over.

"Hi, J.D." She lifted a hand to shade her eyes as she looked up at him. "What brings you to our part of the country?"

With her hair all twisted up in a knot on her head and her cheeks kissed by the sun, she looked more like a teenager than the mother of a set of twins. He shrugged, suddenly feeling self-conscious. "Oh, just thought I'd drop by and see what you and the kids were up to."

He made it sound so casual, as if he'd just zipped across town rather than driven the fifty-plus miles that separated their homes. And on a holiday weekend no less. But Joanie was no fool. No matter what explanation he offered, she knew darn good and well that guilt had prompted the trip.

"As the kids said, we've been to the lake."

He looked up, squinting at the cloudless blue sky. "Well, you definitely had a pretty day for it."

Joanie sighed, a combination of sand and sweat and too much sun shadowing her opinion of the day. "Pretty, but tiring." She motioned for the kids. "Come on, guys, let's get our things into the house." She glanced up at J.D. "Would you like to come inside with us?"

"If I'm not interrupting anything."

Though seeing J.D. again was an unexpected pleasure after their last confrontation, Joanie thought longingly of the shower and nap she'd planned.

"No, nothing. In fact, if you twist my arm, I might be persuaded to make us all some lemonade."

J.D. grinned, taking the picnic basket from her. "I'm pretty good at arm twisting."

She led the way back into the house, waiting while Shane and Marissa retrieved the cooler and the beach bag from the driveway. In the kitchen, she set the picnic basket aside and went immediately to the refrigerator, then the pantry, gathering the ingredients for lemonade. "Why don't you kids run and take a quick bath and change into clean clothes?"

"Do we have to?" Marissa whined.

Joanie looked down her nose at them both. "Yes, and if you hurry, you can be done before the lemonade is ready. And no water fights," she called to their retreating backs.

"What can I do?"

Joanie glanced over at J.D., surprised by his offer. "Well, I suppose you could cut the lemons in half for me." She scooted the cutting board to the side, making room for him at the counter, then handed him a knife.

They worked side by side, J.D. slicing, Joanie squeezing, their arms occasionally brushing as they worked. Each touch was like hitting an electric fence and J.D. wondered if Joanie felt the jolts, as well.

Trying to ignore the effect her nearness had on him, J.D. sliced the last lemon, then turned, propping a hip against the counter as he watched Joanie continue to squeeze the lemons.

Mesmerized by her rhythmic movements, he couldn't help but notice the way the muscles tightened up and down the length of her arm as she squeezed the lemons through the press. Something about the action seemed unreasonably sensual, bringing memories of the feel of those hands slick with passion moving over his heated skin. The thoughts were unsettling and he shifted, putting a little more distance between them. He nodded toward her arm, hoping to get his mind off the lustful thoughts building. "Looks like you got some sun."

Joanie paused in her squeezing to look down at her arm. "Yeah," she said then went back to her squeezing. "A little."

"The kids seemed to have had a good time," he said, needing to fill the awkward silence.

"They usually do. They look forward all year to Serena's Labor Day Picnic."

J.D. frowned, the name sounding familiar. "Serena? Wasn't that the lady who was with you in San Antonio?"

"One and the same." Joanie took the juice and poured it into a pitcher, then moved around J.D. to fill it with water from the sink. "We've been friends for years."

J.D. wasn't sure what made him want to know, but couldn't help asking. "Does she know?"

Joanie jerked her head up to look at him and knew by his solemn expression that he was referring to her pregnancy. She dipped her head, heat flooding her cheeks, and turned off the water. "Yes, she knows. So do my parents," she added, turning to look at him. "I called them a couple of days ago and told them."

He nodded slowly. "I suppose they would have to be told eventually."

She felt tears burn her eyes at his bleak expression. Knowing how much he liked and respected her par-

ents, and how concerned he must be about their reaction to the news, she forced the tears back and laid
a comforting hand on his arm. "Don't worry. They
aren't angry with you. I told them that you offered to
marry me and I also told them that I refused."

"What did they say to that?"

Joanie chuckled. "They know how stubborn I am,
so they didn't try to dissuade me. They just told me
that they would help out financially if I needed them
to."

Embarrassed, J.D. glanced away, guilt eating at him.
"You don't have to worry about money, Joanie," he
said uneasily. "I'll take care of whatever needs you
have."

Joanie sighed, seeing how difficult all of this was
for him. The visit today was proof enough of his concern. "I know that, J.D.," she said softly. "And when
and if the time comes that I need your help, I'll let
you know."

Chapter Five

Fresh from their baths, Marissa and Shane climbed up on stools at the breakfast bar while Joanie placed glasses of lemonade in front of them.

She took the two remaining glasses and set them on the kitchen table. "How's your leg?" she asked as she pulled out a chair.

J.D. dragged out the one opposite hers, spun it around and straddled it. He laid his forearms along the chair's back, picked up the glass and dangled it in the circle of his thumb and finger. "Fine. Half the time, I forget it's broken."

She gave him a knowing look over the top of her glass. "And the other half?"

"It throbs like a—" He cut a glance in the kids' direction and saw that they were hanging on his every word. He swallowed back the crude description he'd been about to offer and said instead, "Let's just say it hurts."

Joanie chuckled and took a sip. "Nice sidestepping," she murmured, her eyes dancing with laughter.

J.D. just grinned.

"Mama, I'm hungry," Shane complained.

"Me, too," Marissa chimed in.

"Hungry!" Joanie repeated, looking at them in surprise. "But you just ate!"

"That was hours ago. We're starving."

J.D. saw Joanie's shoulders slump and knew she must be exhausted after spending a day in the sun. "I saw a pizza place when I was passing through town. Why don't I take the kids and go pick up a pizza while you get a shower?"

Though tempted, Joanie shook her head. "That isn't necessary, really. I have the makings for sandwiches in the fridge."

"Sandwiches," the twins moaned in unison. "Again?"

J.D. chuckled and rose, twirling the chair back into place under the table. "My sentiments exactly. Come on, kids," he said. "I'll treat you to a pizza." He picked up his hat from the counter, then waited until the twins had clambered down from their stools. At the back door, he paused, glancing over at Joanie. "I figure you've got a good hour. Why don't you take a bubble bath and put up your feet?"

Joanie looked at him gratefully. "Thanks, J.D."

Joanie knew how to take advantage of an opportunity when one presented itself. As soon as the back door closed behind the three, she raced down the hall, yanking the sundress over her head. She filled the tub with deliciously warm water, added a large dose of rose-scented foaming bath salts, then eased her tired body into the bubbles. On a sigh, she lay back and closed her eyes.

Thoughts of J.D. pushed through the fog of weariness that weighed on her. *Why did he drive all this way on a holiday weekend just to check on us?* she wondered, then shook her head at the ridiculousness of the question. She knew why he'd made the drive. Guilt could be a mighty strong motivator.

She sighed again and slipped deeper into the bubbles, letting the warm water work on her aching muscles. But no matter what his reason in making the trip, she was glad he was there. Besides the obvious fact that she had just gained an hour of alone time, she was grateful for the opportunity to see J.D.

Tears burned behind her closed eyes and she squeezed her lids even tighter in an attempt to hold the emotions back. No matter how foolish or futile her feelings were, she knew she loved the man.

A sob rose and she choked it down. Love. A heartbreaking emotion when it only traveled one way. And J.D. didn't love her, she knew that. He was an honorable man; his actions proved that. But a man in love? No, Joanie didn't harbor any doubts about his feelings for her. She drew a shuddery breath and the bubbles shifted on her breasts.

As difficult as it would be, she knew she would have to be careful around him to keep her feelings hidden away in her heart.

* * *

J.D. opened the back door. "Joanie?" he called softly.

Not feeling the same compunction J.D. felt on entering the house unannounced, Marissa and Shane impatiently wormed their way around him and through the narrow opening he left in the doorway.

"Mama!" they called in unison, racing into the kitchen. "We're home!"

Joanie stepped into the room wearing the rosebud-covered robe J.D. had first seen her wear at his farm, a towel wrapped turban-style around her damp hair. Though she still looked tired to J.D., she wore a welcoming smile as she dropped to her knees, catching both her kids around their waists and hugging them to her. "And how was the pizza?" she asked.

Marissa wriggled from her arms and ran to grab from J.D. the box he was carrying. "Awesome!" she exclaimed, her excitement evident in the bright smile that lit her face. She raced over to Joanie, opening the box and stuck it under her mother's nose. "And we brought some back for you!"

The overpowering smells of onions, peppers, cheeses and spicy tomato sauce fluttered beneath Joanie's nose. She placed a hand in front of her face to push the box away as her stomach began to roll.

J.D. watched the blood drain from Joanie's face and her complexion take on an almost green cast. She stood, her legs unsteady, then slapped a hand over her mouth and bolted from the room.

Marissa closed the lid on the box, her shoulders drooping. She lifted her gaze to J.D., her eyes filled with disappointment. "I guess Mama has a tummy-ache again," she said sadly.

J.D. didn't have much experience with pregnant women, but he'd heard of morning sickness before and knew that it sometimes hit a woman other than just the morning hours.

"Why don't you kids go in and turn on that movie we rented while I go check on your mother?"

"Aren't you going to watch it with us?" Shane asked as he took the sack J.D. offered.

"Yeah, as soon as I make sure your mom's okay."

Once the kids were out of sight, J.D. hauled in a deep breath, not wanting this duty, but not seeing anyone else around old enough or seasoned enough to take it on. Sighing, he headed for the back of the house. He peeked in doors until he found what he was sure was Joanie's room, then crossed to the bathroom. He pressed an ear against the door and listened, hesitant to barge in, knowing that his presence would probably only embarrass her.

He heard the toilet flush, water splash in the sink then shut off. He strained but heard no other sound. When she didn't come out, he tapped on the door.

"Joanie?"

"What?" she replied, her voice muffled.

"Are you okay?" he asked in concern.

When she didn't answer, he pushed open the door. She sat on the toilet seat, her arm hooked over the edge of the sink and her face buried in the crook of her arm.

He stepped into the room, unsure what he should do. "Can I get you anything?" he asked.

A sob shook her shoulders and he felt a sliver of

fear work its way down his spine. He didn't have any experience with a woman's tears. At least not in a situation like this. He hesitated a moment longer, wondering whether he shouldn't just leave her to suffer alone, thinking his presence might just add to her misery.

But he quickly discovered that he couldn't leave, not with her being so sick. He crossed to hunker down at her feet. Bracing a hand on the sink near her arm, he leaned to brush the hair away from her face and tuck it behind her ear. "Morning sickness?" he asked softly.

She nodded, her sobs increasing in strength.

"Is there anything I can do?"

She shook her head, but refused to look at him.

J.D. knelt in silence, stroking his hand down her back in an attempt to soothe her. A thin piece of fabric was all that separated her bare skin from his. Through it he felt the quiver of her flesh, the heave of her shoulders with each drawn breath. He tightened his lips as an emotion washed over him, something he'd never experienced before...compassion. Oh, he may have felt it on occasion, but never so strongly, never so deeply that he wanted to take what pained a person and make it his own.

Slowly, her sobs lessened and she lifted her head, wiping away the trace of tears with shaky hands.

"I'm sorry," she murmured, ducking her head and catching the edges of her robe to drag across her knees. "I feel better now."

J.D. doubted that. Her face was still as white as a sheet and her fingers trembled in the folds of her robe.

He stood, cupping her elbow in his hand. "Why don't you lie down for a while?"

Joanie stood and shook her head. "No, I need to get Marissa and Shane ready for bed. I'll be all right."

J.D. wagged his head at her stubbornness. "I'll see to the kids."

Joanie looked up at him in surprise, her eyes still watery from the tears. "You?"

J.D. scowled to think that she would doubt his ability to deal with two little children. "I think I can handle it," he said dryly.

Though she continued to argue with him—if only halfheartedly—that she was fine and quite able to take care of the twins herself, J.D. ignored her and guided her to the side of her bed. He released his hold on her long enough to throw back the bedspread, then waited while she climbed in.

Taking the covers, he pulled them snugly over her, then switched off her bedside lamp. "Don't worry about the kids," he assured her gently. "I'll take care of them." He left the room, closing the door softly behind him.

When he returned an hour later to check on her, she was sleeping soundly.

Joanie awakened and rolled to her back, moaning, knowing she should get up but not wanting to. She opened one eye to glance at the clock. The illuminated dial read eight o'clock. Both eyes flipped open with a start. Eight o'clock! She never slept this late! Marissa and Shane were probably up and wanting their breakfast. Her thoughts quickly flicked to the night before and J.D.'s offer to put the two to bed. Bolting up, she barreled down the short hall to check on them.

When she found their room empty, she knew a moment's panic as she raced for the den. There she found them on the floor, snuggled together on a pallet of quilts in front of the dark television screen, sleeping. With a hand pressed to her pounding heart, she touched a finger to her lips then to each head, grateful to find them safe.

Not that she thought J.D. was incapable of caring for them, she assured herself as she glanced around the room, but she was a mother, a protective one, and had been solely responsible for their safekeeping for so long that it was hard to entrust anyone else with their care.

On the coffee table she found a half-empty bowl of popcorn, a cardboard pizza box and three empty cola cans. The third can made her hopeful that J.D. had still been in her house when her two children had decided to throw a late-night party. Chuckling softly, she gathered the remnants of their feast and headed for the kitchen.

When she pushed through the swinging door that led to the kitchen, she stopped, sucking in a startled breath. J.D. sat at the kitchen table, his chest bare, his lips puckered as he blew on a mug of steaming coffee to cool it. The morning paper was spread on the table beneath his elbows. His hair was mussed, his feet bare, and he looked so at home at her kitchen table and so incredibly handsome that Joanie felt a lump of emotion tighten in her throat.

When the door rocked back on its hinges behind her with a squeak, J.D. glanced up, his lips still pursed.

His gaze touched hers briefly before dropping to her hands. He cringed at the sight of the items she carried. "Oops," he murmured guiltily. "You caught us before I had a chance to hide the evidence."

Joanie simply stared. "You spent the night?" she asked in disbelief.

"Yeah. When I went back to check on you, you were asleep. To be on the safe side, I decided to just sack out on the sofa."

J. D. Cawthon on her sofa? Joanie didn't quite know what to think of this.

When she continued to stand at the door, staring, a self-conscious grin chipped at one corner of his mouth. He held up the mug of coffee. "Hope you don't mind. I made myself at home."

Flustered to learn that he'd actually slept in her house without her knowledge, Joanie mumbled an unintelligible response and crossed to the sink. She dumped the empty containers in the wastebasket, then turned on the tap to rinse out the popcorn bowl.

"Are you feeling better this morning?"

Joanie felt heat flood her cheeks. He'd witnessed her sickness, seen her at her most vulnerable, hugging the toilet. She set the bowl aside to drain, keeping her back to J.D. "Much better, thank you." She caught up a towel and turned to him, drying her hands, hoping her embarrassment didn't show. "I appreciate your taking care of the children."

"They weren't any trouble."

In spite of her embarrassment, Joanie chortled, knowing he was only being kind. Her children were basically good kids, but they could smell a sucker a mile away. "How long did it take them to convince you to let them camp out in the den?"

It was J.D.'s turn to blush. "Well," he replied hesitantly, "they didn't seem to be too sleepy, so I let them make a pallet on the floor, hoping that a movie would put them to sleep."

"I bet that took awhile, considering they were wired."

"Wired?" he repeated, frowning.

"I don't allow them to have any caffeine after dinner."

"What caffeine?"

Joanie laughed again. "The cola. It's loaded with it."

J.D. grimaced. "Sorry. I didn't think about that."

Joanie reached for a mug and filled it with coffee. "Don't worry," she said, pausing long enough to give him a consoling pat on the shoulder before sitting opposite him at the table. "They usually test every baby-sitter to see what they can get by with."

Baby-sitter? J.D. had been called a lot of things in his life, but never a baby-sitter. He wasn't at all sure he liked the tag.

"Although," Joanie added, raising one brow, "most of their baby-sitters are closer to sixteen than thirty-three and usually manage to keep their clothes on."

J.D. self-consciously laid a hand on his chest and rubbed it as if only now realizing his state of undress. "Never liked sleeping in my clothes," he mumbled.

Joanie just chuckled and took another sip of her coffee. "I'm surprised that you slept at all. I would imagine that sofa is about a foot short of being comfortable for a man your size.''

"I've slept on worse.''

Joanie nodded her head in agreement, knowing from her brother George's experience what riding the rodeo circuit was like. "I'm sure you have.'' She caught her cup between her hands, her expression suddenly serious. "Why did you come here, J.D.?''

He shuffled his bare feet under the table, uncomfortable with the question. "Like I said, to check on y'all.''

A hint of a smile softened the corners of Joanie's mouth. "Although that's really sweet, it's unnecessary.''

J.D. frowned, his shoulders stiffening defensively. "Looked to me like I came at just the right time. Who'd have taken care of the kids for you if I hadn't been here?''

"I'd have managed. I've been doing the job all of their lives.''

Her response made him think of the kids' dad. "Doesn't their father ever help out?''

Joanie sighed, turning her face to the kitchen window. "No.'' She stared a moment, her eyes filled with what J.D. could only term regret. "Josh moved to California after our divorce. Distance alone would make it difficult for him to take a very active role in their lives, although he does visit now and then.''

J.D. heard what she didn't say. "But distance isn't the only factor,'' he returned.

Joanie turned to look him, her face tight with carefully controlled emotion. "No, distance isn't the only factor.'' She sighed, letting the anger go as quickly as it had come, and turned her gaze to her coffee mug. "Josh didn't adapt well to fatherhood," she admitted, then chuckled ruefully as she slowly turned the mug in her hands. "In fact, Marissa and Shane scared him to death. He didn't have a clue how to respond to them and, to be honest, never really made much of an attempt."

Not knowing what to say, J.D. sat in silence, waiting for her to go on.

"In retrospect, we should never have married," she said with regret, "much less had children. Josh avoided commitment, whether it was to our marriage or to his children or even to a job."

"Doesn't he help with their support?"

Joanie slowly shook her head. "No, not really. Occasionally, he'll have an attack of conscience and send us a check. But those times are rare."

"Couldn't you sue him for child support?"

Joanie shrugged. "I could," she replied, then added, "but I won't."

"Why not?"

"To start with, the legal hassle involved. But more importantly, I feel whatever he contributes to their care should come from his heart, not from some judge forcing his compliance."

J.D. glanced at Joanie's stomach and felt his own guilt rise as he thought of his reasons for coming to Liberty Hill. Granted, he'd wanted to check on Joanie and see if she needed anything, but he knew his offer didn't come any more from his heart than the absent Josh's occasional check.

He had no feelings for the baby that grew inside Joanie. Truth be known, he was still having a difficult time accepting the fact that he had fathered a child. There was nothing substantial to confirm his participation, nothing to see, nothing to put his hands on to give the situation any sense of reality.

Not that he doubted Joanie's word. He didn't. But he was a man who dealt with facts, not fantasy. And for now, at least, the baby that secretly grew inside her was more fantasy than fact.

Tears blurring her vision, Joanie picked up the one-hundred-dollar bill from the kitchen counter and curled her fingers around it as she drew it to her heart. The kindness in the gesture touched her as nothing else could. She crossed to the window and looked out just in time to see J.D.'s truck pull away from the curb.

That he hadn't mentioned the money didn't surprise her. It would be like J.D. to leave it for her to find rather than give it to her outright. He probably assumed she wouldn't have accepted it...which she wouldn't have if he'd offered it first. She didn't need his help. At least, not yet.

She watched until his truck disappeared around a turn, then tucked the money into her pocket, saving it for the day when she would.

With school back in session, Joanie's and her children's days quickly fell into a routine they were all familiar with— rising at six, a quick breakfast together, then off to school. With the twins in kindergarten now, Joanie didn't have to worry about full-time day care any longer, only the hour at the end of the day when their school schedules differed.

Earlier in the summer, she'd made arrangements

with a neighbor to pick up the children at three and keep them with her at her home until Joanie got off work at four. Marissa and Shane usually spent the remainder of the afternoon playing outside while Joanie graded papers at the kitchen table and cooked dinner.

The only kink in the schedule was with Joanie and her decreased energy level due to her pregnancy. By the time she arrived home, she was exhausted from standing on her feet all day and wanted nothing more than a nice cozy nap. She knew from experience that the fatigue would pass, but until it did, she had to give a wide berth to the sofa and its temptation as she crossed the living room on her way to the kitchen.

In the past, weekends during the school year were spent catching up on housekeeping chores and laundry, with a wild dash through the grocery store tossed in to refill the refrigerator and pantry for the next week's meals. But a kink in that schedule soon presented itself, as well. That kink came in the form of J. D. Cawthon.

Saturday morning, Joanie was in the driveway, buckling the twins into their seat-belts for the trip to the grocery store when a truck pulled across the end of the drive. Joanie glanced up to see J.D. climb from the cab. Dressed in jeans, a denim shirt and scuffed ropers he strolled up the driveway, looking as handsome as the devil himself. Her heart kicked against her ribs at the sight of him, but she quickly stilled it by reminding herself that his unexpected visit wasn't a social call, but one made out of a sense of duty.

He stopped beside her, hooked his thumbs through his belt loops and looked down at her, a half grin teasing the corner of his mouth. "Are y'all coming or going?"

In spite of her attempts to remain unaffected, Joanie felt herself smiling into eyes as blue as the sky above. "Going. We're on our way to do some grocery shopping."

"Mind if I tag along?"

Though she couldn't imagine why J.D. would want to go shopping with them, she shrugged. "Suit yourself."

It must have suited him because, without another word, he rounded the hood of the car and climbed in, folding his long legs beneath the dash of her compact car. Once settled, he draped an arm along the back of the seat and twisted around to look behind him. "Hi, kids. How was your first full week of school?"

That one question carried the conversation all through the drive to the store, then up and down its aisles while Joanie shopped for the items on her list. At the checkout, J.D. waited patiently while the cashier rang up their purchases, then quietly shouldered Joanie out of the way when she reached for her purse.

Stunned, Joanie stood staring while he pulled out his wallet and paid for her groceries, then hefted Marissa up and stuffed her in the cart along with the sacks. "You climb on below, cowboy," he ordered Shane, then proceeded to push the loaded cart through the double doors and out to the parking lot.

Joanie ran to catch up.

"J.D., you're not paying for our food," she admonished him.

He plucked the keys from her hand and opened the

trunk. "Why not?" he asked as he began shifting sacks from the cart to the trunk.

"Because…" Flustered, Joanie struggled to think of a reason. "Because you're not eating the food. We are."

J.D. slammed down the trunk lid, then scooped Marissa out of the cart and into his arms. He looked at the little girl, his expression woeful. "I guess that means I don't get any dinner, huh, kiddo?" he said, then shifted a pitiful gaze to Joanie.

Marissa threw a protective arm around his shoulder. "Sure you do, J.D.," she assured him, patting him consolingly. "Mama didn't mean what she said." She glanced at her mother for confirmation. "Did you, Mama?"

From that Saturday on, J.D.'s visits became a weekly ritual that Marissa and Shane grew to look forward to…and Joanie tried her best not to. He never came empty-handed. He always brought something, whether it was a sack of vegetables from Lupe and Manuel's garden, or steaks to cook out on the grill.

Joanie tried to convince him that his visits weren't expected and his gifts unnecessary, but he continued to show up like clockwork every Saturday morning, prepared to spend the day. He mowed her yard, changed the oil in her clunker of a car and even played baseball with Marissa and Shane.

Though Joanie knew that everything he did, he did out of a sense of guilt, his actions, especially those directed at her children, touched her heart in a way money never could.

* * *

Two bald light bulbs swung from the ceiling of the old barn, casting light on the flatbed trailer where Joanie worked stuffing paper flowers through chicken wire. A width of red corrugated cardboard skirted the edge of the flatbed trailer which was already hooked up to the John Deere tractor that would pull it during the Liberty Hill Fall Festival parade. The skeleton of a huge panther shaped from chicken wire stood in the middle of the platform. Joanie knelt at the side of the panther, poking black paper flowers through the small metal circles. Her muscles ached from the tedious work and her fingers throbbed from pricks made by the wire.

Propped on a hay bale nearby, a boom box filled the cavernous room with pulsing rap music. About a dozen teenagers, doing what teenagers do best, milled around the room, talking and laughing and flirting, but accomplishing little. Joanie pressed a hand to her forehead, silently wishing the batteries in the boom box would die. Her children were home with a baby-sitter and hopefully by now in bed, which was exactly where she wanted to be…home in bed.

But with the Liberty Hill Festival parade scheduled for ten o'clock the next morning and the high school's float not even half-finished, Joanie knew bedtime for her was still a long way off.

As the sponsor for her school's entry in the parade, she was the only adult within a mile of the barn and she knew it was up to her to get the kids cracking or the float would never be finished on time.

She raised her voice to be heard over the blasting music. "Okay, guys, come on, I need help stuffing this panther. Julie, bring me that sack of black flowers that's sitting by the tractor wheel. Jennifer and Ashley, you girls need to make more white flowers. Jerrod and Mickey, set up the ladder in front of the backdrop and let's start filling in the color for the scene.''

Though they did so reluctantly, the students followed her instructions. When the boys had the ladder in place, Joanie stood, placing her hands in the middle of her back and stretching, stiff after kneeling in the same position for so long. Working her way carefully through the maze of decorations littering the floor of the trailer, she headed for the ladder.

"Let's stuff the blue for the sky first, then follow with the green for the trees.''

Jerrod rocked back on his heels at the foot of the ladder and frowned as he stared up at the expanse of chicken wire. "How do you know what's sky and what's trees?"

Joanie heaved a frustrated sigh and grabbed a sack of blue tissue flowers. "You hold the ladder and I'll outline the sky,'' she told him as she stepped onto the first rung, tucking the sack beneath her arm. "Then you can fill in the rest.''

The backdrop stretched a good ten feet in the air above her. Gingerly, Joanie climbed to the top of the ladder, placed the sack on the pail rest, then plucked out a flower. Gripping the side rail with her knees, she leaned over and began twisting the flowers through the wire mesh. When she had filled as many as she could reach, she shifted her weight to step down a level. But as she lowered her foot, the ladder rocked precariously.

"Hey, Jerrod," she called anxiously, "hold it

steady.'' When the ladder continued to wobble, she glanced down to see that Jerrod was nowhere in sight.

She made a wild grab for the backdrop to stick her fingers through the mesh in order to regain her balance, but when she did, the ladder pitched wildly to the left. Joanie felt herself slipping and clawed frantically, searching for something to hang on to…but there was nothing between her and the wooden platform but air. Just before her body slammed against the trailer's floor, her chin struck the ladder's side rail stunning her. The wind was knocked out of her lungs in a whoosh as she landed and a wrenching pain tore through her back.

Oh, my God, the baby!

That was Joanie's last thought before darkness swallowed her.

J.D. sat parked in front of Joanie's house, slumped behind the steering wheel. He'd been waiting for what seemed like hours for her to return. When he'd first arrived, he'd knocked at the door and been greeted by a young girl who introduced herself as the baby-sitter. With the screen door securely locked between them, she'd told J.D. that the kids were already asleep and Joanie was away supervising the building of a float for the parade the next day and wasn't expected back for another hour yet. Seeing that his presence made the girl nervous, J.D. told her that he would just wait in his truck until Joanie returned.

Now he was wishing he'd simply turned around and driven the fifty miles back to his farm. He sighed and shifted, trying to find a more comfortable position. His rear end was numb from sitting so long. He was tempted to knock on the door, pay the girl what was owed her and do the rest of his waiting stretched out on Joanie's sofa. But he knew the girl would never go for that. She didn't have a clue who he was and he could tell by the suspicious look she'd given him that she would never let him in the front door, much less pass the responsibility of the kids on to him.

He frowned at the darkness through the windshield. He usually made his visits to check on Joanie and the kids on Saturdays, but tomorrow he had a man coming who wanted to use J.D.'s stud for breeding, so he thought he'd make the trip tonight, see if they were doing okay, then hightail it back for home. A sigh shuddered through him. He certainly hadn't intended to spend the night sitting in his truck.

A squeal of tires behind him had him glancing at the rearview mirror. A set of headlights blinded him momentarily before the car raced past him, then careened into Joanie's drive, taking the turn on two wheels.

"What the hell," he muttered under his breath, his fingers already curling around the door handle. By the time the driver stepped from the car, J.D. was already striding across the lawn. In the glow from the porch light, he saw that the driver was a woman and he recognized her as the friend who'd accompanied Joanie that night in San Antonio.

She stopped when she saw him and he could see by the look on her face that something was wrong. *Joanie. Something had happened to Joanie.* Fear tightened his chest as he closed the distance between them at a run. "Where's Joanie?" he demanded, grabbing her arm. "What's happened to her?"

Serena jerked away from him, and he was surprised to see accusation in her eyes. "She's in the hospital."

J.D. felt his knees weaken. "Hospital! Is she hurt?"

"Not badly. But the doctor is making her stay overnight for observation."

"But what happened?"

"She was climbing a ladder—"

"A ladder!" he all but roared. "What in the hell was she doing on a ladder in her condition?"

"She was earning her salary," Serena replied resentfully, and J.D. knew then that she blamed him for Joanie's accident. "She's the sponsor of the high school's entry in the parade tomorrow and she was helping decorate the float."

J.D.'s face paled as a new thought formed. "The baby?"

Serena's gaze hardened. "A little late for your concern, isn't it?" she asked.

J.D.'s face tightened, his jaw muscle convulsing. He knew he deserved the verbal slap, but that didn't make it any easier to accept. "Where is she?"

"At the hospital in Georgetown." Before the words were even out of her mouth, he had bolted and was running for his truck. Serena yelled after him, "It won't do any good to drive over there. They won't let you see her!"

"Let 'em try to stop me," J.D. muttered as he climbed into his truck.

Chapter Six

The nurse sitting guard at the nurses' station looked more like a drill sergeant than an angel of mercy, but J.D. had been up against stronger odds. He simply turned on the charm.

"Evenin', ma'am," he said, dragging off his hat and holding it humbly at his waist. "Could you tell me what room Joanie Summers is in?"

The nurse didn't even look up but kept scribbling on a chart in front of her. "Visiting hours are over. You'll have to come back tomorrow."

J.D. eased closer to the desk. "I know that, but I just arrived in town. I was hoping I could see her tonight."

"Well, you can't," she snapped impatiently. "She needs her rest."

J.D. stood a moment, shifting from one foot to the

other, frustration warring with a need for patience. "Yes, ma'am, I'm sure she does, and I can promise you I won't disturb her. I just need to see her. To see for myself that she's all right."

The woman glanced up, frowning. "Are you family?"

"No, ma'am. Just a friend."

She gave him a sideways glance. "You wouldn't happen to be the father of that baby she's carrying, now would you?"

Father? Hearing the word voiced out loud shook J.D. clear to the bone. He'd never discussed the baby or its impending birth with anyone other than Joanie. Doing so now painted a layer of realism on his approaching fatherhood that had been missing before. He hauled in a deep breath and looked her straight in the eye. "Yes, ma'am, I am. Is the baby all right?"

"You'll have to talk to the doctor about that." She continued to study him, her mouth puckered into a frown. Something she saw in his expression must have softened her a little, because she waved him away with her hand. "Oh, all right," she said grumpily. "You can see her. But only for a few minutes. She's in room 101."

Letting out a relieved sigh, J.D. mumbled a "thank you, ma'am" and headed down the hall. He pushed open the door to Joanie's room and stuck in his head. A night-light glowed above the bed, silhouetting Joanie. She lay on her back, her eyes closed, her chest rising and falling beneath the crisp white sheet in the even rhythm of sleep.

He stepped farther into the room, letting the door swish closed behind him. He laid his hat on the bedside table, then eased closer to the bed, wanting to make good his promise to the nurse and not wake her. Needing to see for himself that she was unhurt, he bent over to brace a hand on either side of her. The scent of roses drifted just beneath his nose. Her eyes were closed, her lashes feathering her cheekbones. She looked like an angel, sleeping so peacefully, her hair a blond halo around her face.

His heart pushed its way to his throat, and he had a hard time swallowing it back. He didn't know when this woman had grown to mean so much to him, but at the moment, he wanted nothing more than to gather her in his arms and hold her close.

Instead, he lightly brushed a wisp of hair from her face, satisfying himself with that slight physical contact. At his touch, she sighed softly, turning her cheek against the back of his hand and nuzzling. J.D. was sure he'd never experienced anything in his life that moved him so deeply.

But as he took in the bandage that covered the left side of her chin and the angry red scrape that cut across her forehead, hot tears burned behind his eyes.

He gathered her hand into his as he sank into the chair beside the bed, his knees suddenly feeling as if they were filled with water.

Joanie, oh, Joanie, he intoned silently, emotion clotting his throat, *please be all right.*

Joanie awakened, feeling as if she'd been run over by a Mac truck. She moaned softly and tried to shift to a more comfortable position. Unfortunately, there wasn't one. Her entire body ached from head to toe.

Touching a hand to her chin and feeling the bandage, she pushed herself to a sitting position and immediately reached for the phone, wanting to check on Serena and the twins. Along with hard plastic, her hand grazed stiff felt. Frowning, she turned her head to look at the cowboy hat beside the phone. A very familiar cowboy hat.

She glanced around, looking for some sign of J.D., but all she found was a bouquet of roses on the bedside table and a cloud of balloons tied to the foot of her bed. He couldn't have been here, she told herself. How could he have known? Yet something nagged at her, a memory that refused to surface.

Letting the receiver drop back onto its cradle, she picked up the hat. Burned into the leather band inside the rim was the message, "Like hell this hat is yours. This Stetson belongs to J. D. Cawthon." She smiled, then winced, touching a finger to her bruised chin.

Drawing up her legs, she propped the hat on her perched knees, wondering how he'd known she was in the hospital. "Serena," she murmured on a resigned sigh. She was the only other person who knew about J.D. She must have called him and told him about the accident. She made a mental note to tell Serena that in the future she was to mind her own business.

At that moment, the door swished open and Joanie glanced toward it. J.D.'s head popped through the narrow opening.

Seeing him sent her pulse racing. Guilt, she told herself. That was the only reason he'd come. Struggling to keep her emotions in check, she held up the hat. "Forget something?"

He stepped inside, looking sheepish. "As a matter

of fact, no, I didn't. I just went down to the cafeteria to grab a bite of breakfast.''

The memory surfaced then, that bit of remembrance that had evaded her earlier. She'd awakened during the night, frightened and alone, and had discovered J.D. beside her, his head resting on their joined hands. His presence had given her a peace, a sense of well-being, of feeling loved and cared for that she hadn't experienced in years. She'd thought then that she was dreaming, but held the vision close to her heart as she drifted back to sleep again.

But now she knew it wasn't a dream and that J.D. must have really spent the night beside her bed. For some silly reason, that same sense of well-being, of feeling cherished stole over her again.

Shyly, she held out the hat to him and he took it, rotating it by its brim.

"How are you feeling?" he asked.

"Sore, but fine otherwise. I'm sorry Serena called you. She shouldn't have."

"She didn't call. I was at the house waiting for you when she came to take care of the kids."

"You were at the house?" she repeated in surprise.

"Yeah. I have a man coming today who wants to breed his mare to my stud, so I thought I'd drive up last night to check on you and the kids instead of today. When the baby-sitter said you'd be back within the hour, I decided just to wait in my truck."

"Oh, J.D., I had no idea. I'm sorry for the inconvenience."

He shook his head, a teasing grin pulling at his mouth. "I'm sure you took that swan dive off the ladder just to inconvenience me."

Joanie grinned back at him. "Yeah, right," she said dryly.

The door opened again and Joanie and J.D. both turned to find Doc Reynolds stepping inside.

"And how's my favorite patient this morning?" he asked, smiling. J.D. stepped back, giving him room.

Joanie offered the doctor a smile in return. "Anxious to get home."

His expression dipped quickly into a frown. "I don't think you'll be going home just yet," he warned as he picked up her wrist to take her pulse.

Joanie's eyes widened. "But I have to go home," she cried. "I have two children to take care of."

Doc Reynolds nodded his head in understanding, keeping his gaze on his watch and its second hand. "I know that you do, Joanie, but you're also carrying another one inside you and that one took a pretty good fall last night along with his mother."

Joanie fought back tears, thinking of the danger she had placed her unborn baby in. She lifted her gaze to his. "The baby's going to be okay, isn't it?"

J.D. found himself holding his breath.

The doctor laid her arm back on the covers and picked up her chart. "That depends on you. You're spotting some, but there doesn't seem to be any damage done." J.D.'s breath came out on a long, relieved sigh. "It's probably just nature's way of warning you to take better care of yourself," the doctor added. He made a notation on the chart. "Another day in the hospital, then I recommend total bed rest for two weeks. After that, you should be able to resume your normal activities." He narrowed an eye at her. "And that doesn't mean swinging from ladders."

"But, Doc—"

J.D. could see how upsetting the idea of spending another night in the hospital away from her kids was to Joanie. He stepped to the foot of the bed. "If she had someone to care for her, would you discharge her?"

Doc Reynolds turned, eyeing J.D. over the top of his bifocals. "Yes, I suppose."

J.D. waved at the chart. "Discharge her, then. I'll see that she follows your orders."

"J.D., this isn't necessary, really!" Joanie argued as he plumped pillows behind her back.

"Doc says it is."

"Doc Reynolds is an old worrywart. I'm perfectly capable of taking care of myself. Besides, you need to get back to your farm and take care of your business."

"Manuel can supervise the breeding. He's done it before."

"But, J.D...."

Ignoring her, he moved to the bathroom and ran water into a glass, then returned, handing it and a pill the doctor had prescribed to her. Joanie took them both, scowling. "This is utterly ridiculous," she fumed before tossing back the pill and washing it down with the water.

"What's ridiculous?" Serena asked, breezing into the room, carrying a lunch tray.

"Staying in bed," Joanie complained.

Serena laughed, setting the tray on Joanie's lap. "Better get used to it, kid."

Joanie looked at the contents of the tray and groaned. "Soup? Did Doc Reynolds order that, too?"

Serena laughed again and perched herself at the foot of the bed, tucking her feet beneath her. "No, that's all I know how to cook."

Joanie grimaced as she sniffed at the bowl. "What is it?"

"It started out as potato soup, but I couldn't find all the ingredients, so I improvised."

Fully aware of her friend's inexperience in the kitchen, she picked up the spoon and took a cautious sip. "What are the kids eating?" she asked, nearly choking after only one taste.

"Hamburgers. We stopped on our way home from the parade and picked them up."

Joanie swallowed quickly at the mention of the parade. "Did the high-school float make it to the parade?"

Serena nodded. "Yes, though I'm afraid they didn't win any ribbons. They seemed to be having difficulty keeping the backdrop in place. I think your fall did some permanent damage. Jerrod and Mickey had to trot behind the trailer, holding it up. Oh, and by the way," she added, "I heard Jerrod feels guiltier than hell about what happened to you."

Joanie dropped her spoon into the bowl, her eyes filled with sympathy. "Poor baby. I'll have to call him. It wasn't his fault."

Serena snorted. "Let him suffer for a while. It'll do him good for leaving you on that ladder unattended."

J.D. listened to the exchange, his neck muscles tensing, silently vowing to look up this Jerrod kid himself.

"Mr. Warner sends his best for a speedy recovery."

Joanie groaned. "The principal knows what happened?"

"*Everybody* knows about your fall."

Joanie stole a surreptitious glance at J.D., then looked back to Serena. "Do they know everything?" she asked in a low voice.

"Everything. You know how those nurses gossip."

Joanie set the tray aside, her appetite gone, and sank back against the headboard. "Oh, no," she murmured.

"They were going to find out eventually anyway. You can't keep something like this a secret forever."

"I know, but I wanted to teach until at least the end of the month."

Serena stood and picked up the tray. "I thought the doctor said you have to stay off your feet for the next couple of weeks?"

Joanie waved away the question. "You know Doc Reynolds. He's an alarmist."

"Mmm-hmm," Serena agreed, placating her. Since she'd decided that her opinion of J.D. might deserve reconsideration after he'd spent the night at the hospital with Joanie, she offered him a small smile before leaving the room.

J.D. hesitated a minute, then crossed to the bed. "Joanie, I think it would be best if you and the kids came home with me."

Joanie couldn't have been any more surprised. "Home with you!" she repeated. "Whatever for?"

J.D. lifted a shoulder in a self-conscious shrug. "So I can look after all of you."

Though her heart swelled until she thought it would burst at the kindness in the offer, she shook her head. "Thanks, J.D., but that isn't necessary. We can make out just fine here at home."

"I'm sure you can," he replied amiably. "But you need to think of the baby."

He saw the spurt of tears to her eyes and noticed the way her hand moved protectively to her stomach and knew that he'd hit the right nerve he needed in order to convince her to see things his way.

"I can't afford to be away from the farm for two weeks," he continued. "And it would be a hell of a lot easier for me to look after all of you if you were there with me. This driving back and forth is wearing a hole in my backside. Besides, Lupe's there, and she can help out with the kids."

"But the children have school."

"We can send them to school in Taylor, or, if you're worried about what folks might say, you can home school 'em."

Joanie bit back a smile. "People will talk no matter where we live. I'm not worried about that."

He perched himself at the foot of her bed and took her hand in his. "Then come live with me. Just until the baby's born," he added, hoping to sway her. "Then you can move back here or wherever else you want to live."

The arrangement wasn't one Joanie truly felt comfortable with, but in all honesty she had to agree that he was right. His trips between his farm and Liberty Hill had increased over the past month, taking much-needed time away from his farm.

But the deciding factor had been the promise of help with the twins. With her confined to bed for two weeks, she knew she couldn't properly care for them, and knew, too, that they would be much happier on

J.D.'s farm. And, as always, Joanie's first concern was for her children.

So, with her supervising and J.D. and Serena doing all the legwork, she took a leave of absence from her teaching job, and packed up her family, kitten and all, and moved.

But knowing she was doing the right thing and liking it, she soon discovered, were two entirely different balls of wax.

After ten days at the farm, spending her days propped up in bed with a clutter of magazines and books spread across her lap, Joanie was bored to tears. At the moment, she could hear Marissa and Shane playing in the yard while Lupe hung wash on the line. The woman was a godsend and she seemed to adore the children, but Joanie was sick to death of being sequestered in this room and in this bed and wanted nothing more than to be outside with her kids.

Tears of frustration burned her eyes.

"Do you need anything?"

Joanie glanced from the window to the doorway and found J.D. standing there. She quickly blinked her eyes to chase away the ungrateful tears. "No, I'm fine," she assured him.

He chuckled, knowing she lied, and walked into the room. "Cabin fever?"

Joanie fisted her hands against the bed-covers to keep from screaming her frustrations. "A little," she conceded.

He sat on the foot of the bed, hitching his jeans a little higher on one knee to cross his legs. "I know I'd go stark raving crazy if I had to lie in bed all day."

Joanie smiled then, plucking at the threads on the quilt that covered the bed as she looked up at him through a web of thick lashes. "I'm past crazy. I'm working on certifiably insane."

J.D. tossed back his head and laughed. The sound warmed Joanie's soul. She couldn't remember ever hearing him laugh before. He'd grinned. Even chuckled a time or two, but he'd never out and out laughed.

"How about if I help you escape?" he offered. "You could ride with me in the truck while I drive down to the far pasture and check on the brood mares. That wouldn't exert you too much, would it?"

Joanie's eyes brightened at the offer. "No, of course it wouldn't!"

He grinned as he stood. "Well, throw on some clothes, then. We're burning daylight."

Joanie was scooting off the bed before the door closed behind him.

Joanie rolled down her window and drew in a deep breath of fresh air as the truck bounced over the uneven terrain.

J.D. cocked his head her way, his forehead puckered in concern. "It isn't too rough, is it?"

Laughing, Joanie let the wind have her hair. "Not in the least."

J.D. grinned. He hadn't seen Joanie this happy since she'd moved to his farm. Funny. He hadn't realized he'd missed her smile until he saw it again. "Enjoying yourself?"

Joanie beamed her pleasure, her smile as bright as the afternoon sun. "Immensely."

"Want to stretch your legs a bit?"

"Do you mind?" she asked hopefully.

In answer, he steered the truck toward a stand of trees. He climbed out, then circled the truck to help her down. "Watch your step," he warned, taking her by the elbow.

When her feet touched the ground, Joanie spun in a slow circle, her head tipped back, her arms flung wide, her face turned to the sky. "Oh, this is glorious," she cried, loving the feel of sunshine on her face after so many days without it.

J.D. chuckled and shook his head. He caught her by the hand. "Come on, let's take a walk."

He led her through the trees, tramping across crisp fall leaves and to the bank of a creek. Water trickled lazily over rocks below them. On the opposite side of the creek, a dozen or more horses grazed in a meadow of lush green winter grass. J.D. whistled and they lifted their heads.

"Oh, they're beautiful," Joanie murmured.

J.D. stood watching them, his chest swelling with pride. He'd worked hard to build this place and he'd chosen his stock with the care most men used in choosing a wife. "Yeah, they are." One of the horses raised her head and nickered. "That's Maizy," he said, lifting a hand and pointing. "She was the first mare I bought."

Joanie heard the pride in his voice. "You chose well."

"I think so. She's dropped some mighty fine colts for me over the past four years." He took her hand again and led her to a limestone boulder that stretched as long as a sofa along the bank. "Let's sit here awhile. We don't want you overdoing it."

The gentleness with which he handled her, touched Joanie, though she considered it unnecessary. She'd never felt better in her life.

When she'd settled on the cool stone, he sat beside her, then stooped to pluck a blade of grass from a clump growing beside the rock. With his elbows resting on his knees, he rolled the blade between his fingers, staring out over his herd.

Though she'd shared his home for over a week, Joanie hadn't seen much of J.D.... at least not alone. He rose at daybreak and breakfasted alone before heading outdoors. Duties in the barn and out on the farm kept him out of the house most of the day. At night he always came to her room to check on her, but the kids were usually there sprawled on her bed, doing their homework or chattering about their day at school and the new friends they had made, monopolizing the conversation.

Being with him now with nothing but a herd of horses in the distance to distract them made Joanie painfully aware of his nearness. His hip rested not a foot away from hers, the muscled length of his thigh paralleling her own. His broad shoulders, looking tense at the moment, were no more than the stretch of a hand away. Heat from his body slowly seeped into hers.

She shivered as she watched the hypnotic spin of the blade of grass between his fingers, remembering the feel of those same fingers on her bare skin. A smattering of dark hair covered the back of his wide hands and the tanned fingers that twirled the blade of grass were long and sure. The strength in them was undeniable. During the week she'd spent on the farm

when his leg was in a cast, she'd seen him lift bales
of hay and throw them as if they were filled with nothing more substantial than air.

But she'd seen the gentleness in those same hands,
too. She'd seen him with his horses, the way he
smoothed a palm down a colt's neck to calm him as
he'd worked him in the arena. She'd even felt that
same tenderness on her own flesh, felt the strength and
passion that hummed beneath his skin, the tenderness
in his touch.

His knee brushed hers as he stooped to pluck another blade of grass. Shock waves raced up her leg,
awakening nerve endings sleeping beneath her skin.
He glanced up as he straightened and their eyes met
and held, green melting into blue. She saw the need
in his eyes, the same need that burned deep within
her.

The blade of grass slipped slowly from his fingers.

"Joanie..."

"J.D...."

Their names blended as did their bodies as J.D.
twisted sideways and took her into his arms. On a low
groan, he cupped his hand around her neck, his gaze
on hers, drawing her face to his. The heat in his blue
eyes forced hers closed. Their lips met and lightning
arced, sending bolts of electricity ricocheting through
her body. This is what she'd wanted, she thought in
wonder. This was what she'd needed, been starved for
all those long weeks of his visits, but hadn't been willing to admit even to herself before now.

She melted against him, her fingers flexing in the
fabric of his shirt. He tightened his hold on her and
muscles bunched beneath her clenched hands. She

opened them, wanting to absorb every nuance of feeling, the strength, the warmth. The kiss deepened, and he prodded her lips apart with his tongue. Joanie felt the stab echo deep within her feminine core. He twisted on the stone until he straddled it, drawing her into the vee he'd created between his legs. The bulge of his hardened manhood pressed against her hip and she reveled in the knowledge that he wanted her as much as she did him.

His hand curved around her neck, then drifted lower, cupping a breast. He drew back then, his gaze on hers, and with trembling fingers unhooked the first two buttons of her sack-like dress. She'd been in such a hurry when she'd thrown on her clothes, she hadn't bothered to put on a bra. Now she was grateful for that lack of restriction.

Flattening a hand against the valley between her breasts, he pushed a placket slowly to the side, his calloused hand rough against her tender skin, until he'd bared a breast. Cool air hit her fevered skin and her nipple tightened into a hard knot beneath his gaze. On a shuddery sigh, he lowered his face, closing his lips over the engorged flesh. He suckled gently at first, then drew her nipple deeper and deeper into his mouth, taking in more and more of her breast.

Helplessly, Joanie dropped her head back as sensations built, layer upon layer, until she thought she'd surely die. Cupping her hands around his head, she held on to him as passion coiled like a tight spring inside her. With each whirl of his tongue, with each nip of his teeth, she felt herself slipping faster and faster toward the edge of insanity, and she twisted her fingers into the long hair at his neck and clung. "J.D.," she cried. "Please..."

But her plea came too late. Shudders racked her body as an explosion the likes of which she'd never experienced before ripped through her. J.D. held her until the shudders ebbed, then slowly released her, smoothing her dress back in place. He gathered her into his arms and held her close.

"I'm sorry," she gasped against his shoulder, her breath still coming in harsh, dragging heaves. "I—"

"Ssshh," he soothed, tightening his hold on her and pressing his lips to her hair. "It's all right."

"But you—"

He eased far enough away to press a finger to her lips. "I'm fine," he murmured, then tipped her face up to his. Passion still darkened her eyes, but he thought he saw a thread of embarrassment there, as well. "Your pleasure is mine, and all that I need," he whispered, then gathered her back into the fold of his arms.

When they returned to the house, J.D. insisted on Joanie's going right back to bed. Though she wanted to argue the point, she quickly discovered that after spending so much time in bed, the short outing had zapped her strength and a nap sounded rather nice...though she would have preferred taking that nap curled against J.D.'s chest.

Later that evening after dinner, Marissa and Shane came in for a visit as was their habit before going to bed. Shane positioned himself at the foot of the bed with a book about the Berenstain Bears, while Marissa rested her head on her mother's stomach and Joanie combed her fingers through her daughter's silky hair.

It was in that relaxed state that J.D. found them.

Joanie glanced up to find him watching them from the doorway. They shared an intimate look over the children's heads, memories of their afternoon together passing silently between them.

Joanie patted a spot beside her on the bed. "Come on in and join us," she invited.

J.D. strolled inside. "Y'all look like a bunch of slugs," he teased, reaching over to ruffle Shane's hair before finding a spot and settling beside Joanie.

Joanie sighed her contentment. Now that J.D. was there, her circle was complete. "We are."

"What are slugs?" Marissa asked, lifting her head.

"They're sort of like snails," Joanie explained. "Basically lazy creatures."

"Yuck!" Curling her nose, Marissa laid her head down again, then popped right back up. "Mama, your tummy's getting fat."

Joanie's cheeks flamed. She hadn't told the children about her pregnancy, knowing a secret like that would be difficult for them to keep. And when they'd moved to J.D.'s farm after the accident, she'd procrastinated even more and blamed the need for the move on her fall.

She knew that now was the time for the truth.

"There's a baby growing there," she said softly.

"Really?" Marissa asked, her eyes growing round.

Joanie couldn't help but smile. She lifted her hand and cupped Marissa's cheek. "Yes, really."

Shane glanced his mother's way. "Who put it there?"

Joanie could feel J.D. tense beside her and was sorry that he'd been caught in this discussion. But she'd never shied from answering her children's questions about sex and babies, knowing that knowledge freely given and in simple enough terms that they could understand would give them a healthy outlook on their own sexuality. She wouldn't avoid this one now.

She cut a glance at J.D., seeking his approval. He dipped his head to his chest and gave her the barest of nods.

"J.D. did."

Marissa turned her gaze on him, her eyes full of innocence. "Does that mean you'll be the baby's daddy?"

J.D. felt as if a horse had just kicked him right in the gut and knocked the wind from him. Though there was no condemnation in the child's expression, a surge of guilt swept through him. Slowly, he nodded his head. "I guess it does," he replied hesitantly, though the concept was so new to him, he still couldn't believe it himself.

"Will that make you our daddy, too?" she asked.

The question came out of the blue and took J.D. by such surprise that he could only stare.

Joanie quickly shook her head, sparing J.D.'s having to respond. "No, sweetheart. You already have a daddy."

Marissa's lips puckered in a pout. "But I want J.D. to be my daddy, too."

J.D. stood at the corral gate, his arms draped over the top, one boot hooked over the bottom rail, staring off into the darkness at nothing. Although the night

was cool, perspiration dotted his forehead and dampened his shirt.

But I want J.D. to be my daddy, too.

Marissa's voice echoed through the silent night,
haunting him with her innocent request.

"Damn!" he swore and dragged his heel from the
rail. With another curse, he strode for the pasture gate.
He opened it and pushed through, pausing only long
enough to latch the gate behind him. His stride was
long as he trudged through the dew-kissed grass, as if
he could outrun the small voice that chased him.

A mare grazing in the soft moonlight lifted her head
and snorted, blowing a greeting. In spite of his troubled thoughts, J.D. smiled. He held out a hand and
slowed his gait as he crossed to her, talking to her
softly.

"Hello, girl," he murmured, rubbing his hand along
her muzzle. She pushed at his hand, looking for a treat.
He chuckled. "Sorry, Windclaimer, I didn't bring you
anything tonight."

He continued to rub her, moving his hands up to
scratch the spot between her ears, and his thoughts
shifted once again to Marissa. He could see the child's
innocent face, even now, tipped expectantly to his, her
eyes full of what he could only describe as hope when
she'd asked if he would be her daddy, too.

A sigh shuddered through him. He'd made a mistake, a big one. He should never have brought Joanie
and her kids to his farm. He hadn't meant to create
any false hopes in any of them; he'd only wanted to
give Joanie the help he knew was her due. He certainly
didn't want her kids thinking of him as a replacement
for their dad.

Hell, he told himself, they were just a couple of rugrats, a pair of snotty-nosed kids, and he'd never had any desire to be anyone's dad. Kids spelled responsibility with a capital *R* and J.D. had all the responsibility he could handle right here on his farm. He wouldn't allow them to get under his skin or anywhere near his heart. Not now, not when he was so close to making the farm a success. He couldn't.

The mare put her nose to his side and gave him an impatient shove. He stumbled away a couple of steps, then turned back to her, frowning. She lifted her head and nickered, shaking her head as if scolding him.

"Okay, okay," he admitted reluctantly. "So maybe I do like the little rugrats. But I sure as hell don't want them thinking of me as their dad. A friend, maybe," he added after a moment's thought. "But that's it."

What about the child you fathered? How will that child think of you?

He shook his head at his prodding conscience. He had no feelings for the baby that Joanie carried. To him, it was still some indefinable something that existed beyond his realm of comprehension, not anything he could see or touch. He would provide for it, he knew. But care about it? He shook his head again. No, that was still too much in the future for him to even worry about now.

And what about their mother, then? What will you be to her?

Already turning away, J.D. froze midstep.

Joanie? What was she to him? he asked himself, unable to shake off the question. A friend? A lover? Another thought surfaced and he shoved it back. No, he told himself sternly and headed for the house. He wouldn't allow himself to think like that. He'd made one offer of marriage and she'd turned him down flat. And though her refusal had momentarily wounded his ego a little, he'd felt nothing since but relief.

He didn't want a family, he told himself. He had his farm. And his farm was all J.D. had ever wanted.

Chapter Seven

"But why can't we go trick-or-treating?" Shane whined.

"Because there aren't any houses out here," Joanie explained patiently.

"But it's Halloween!" Marissa cried. "We always go trick-or-treating on Halloween."

"I know that, sweetheart," Joanie replied. "But this year we're just going to have to miss it."

J.D. stepped through the back door, dragging off his hat. "Miss what?" he asked as he stopped to hang his hat on a peg by the door.

Marissa folded her arms across her chest in a pout. "We don't get to go trick-or-treating this year. Mama won't let us."

J.D. looked at Joanie and she rolled her eyes. "They've always trick-or-treated in our neighborhood," she explained for his benefit. "But since we don't have a neighborhood, we'll just have to miss this year," she replied, looking pointedly at her children.

J.D. glanced from Marissa to Shane, noting the disappointment on their faces. He'd never gone trick-or-treating himself for he'd grown up on a farm as remote as the one he now lived on. But he remembered well the excitement that day drew for the kids who'd lived in town. They'd return to school the next day with sacks filled with candy and stories of their hair-raising adventures. He felt a stab of sympathy for the twins, knowing the humiliation of not having tales of his own to share. He wouldn't let the kids suffer through that just because they were stuck out on his farm.

"Just because you can't go trick-or-treating doesn't mean you can't have a good time," he said.

Marissa and Shane both looked at him doubtfully.

"How about a hayride?" he asked, dropping to one knee in front of the two. He didn't know where the idea came from. His daddy had certainly never taken him and his brothers and sisters on one, which in some way comforted him, knowing this was a friendly offer, not a "daddy" thing. "We can hitch the wagon to the tractor, pile it high with hay and take a ride through the pastures. We might even build a campfire and cook hot dogs. What do you say?"

The shift from disappointment to excitement was swift. Both children turned to look at their mother hopefully. "Can we, Mama? Can we?"

Joanie just shook her head, laughing. Once again, J.D. had saved the day. "I guess so," she replied, offering J.D. a grateful look.

* * *

It took a while to load the wagon and hook it up to the tractor, but by the time J.D. had finished, Joanie and the twins had packed a basket with food. With the three sitting on blankets spread on the hay, J.D. took them on a bouncy ride across the pasture in the growing dusk, heading toward what he called Salt Rock. No grass grew in the small area, the land almost a solid sheet of limestone, the safest place he could think to build a fire.

Once there, he tossed down a couple of extra bales to use as chairs, then instructed Marissa and Shane to gather wood. While they searched for kindling, he started putting together the makings for a fire. By the time the sun had set, a small fire blazed on Salt Rock.

The twins made quick work of the hot dogs Joanie had packed, grilling them over the fire with wire clothes hangers for skewers, then gulping them down, anxious to get to the real treat, toasting marshmallows for s'mores.

"Don't hold your marshmallow too close to the fire, or it'll burn," J.D. warned as he adjusted Marissa's wire hanger over the dying embers. Once her hand was steady in place, he sat on the ground and scooted backward until his hips rested between Joanie's feet and his back against her bale of hay.

Her hand lighted on his shoulder and squeezed. She leaned her face close to his ear, bringing with her the ever-present scent of roses to blend with the smell of the burning mesquite. "Thanks, J.D.," she murmured. "They'll never forget this night."

Her touch sent heat spreading through his chest and along with it a sense of satisfaction that he had taken what would have been a disappointing evening for the kids and turned it into a memorable one. A friendly gesture, he reminded himself, nothing more than he would do for any other kids stuck out on his farm on Halloween night.

But the heat that slowly worked its way through his body was anything but friendly, bringing with it memories of the afternoon on the rock and the pleasure he'd given Joanie…and the frustrations that had haunted his steps in the days since. He lifted his own hand to cover hers, unable to resist even that slight contact. "No thanks needed," he replied, his voice husky.

Their fingers laced and held. He felt the trembling in her hand and knew his own wasn't much steadier. Too much lay between them, unanswered, unfulfilled. And with the kids close by, things would remain that way.

The temptation to close his eyes and let his head drift back against her was overpowering. He leaned back, cushioning his head between her full breasts and her hands slid around to rest on his chest. The vision came quickly, settling behind his closed lids like a movie projected on a screen. The vision was a familiar one, the same one he'd taken to bed with him every night since the afternoon on the rock.

Joanie was sitting before him, bared to the waist, her breasts washed in sunshine as she arched toward him. Moisture glistened from nipples swollen with the passion that he'd stroked from her. The vision was so clear to him he could almost taste the honeyed sweetness, feel the pebbled texture of her breasts on his tongue, hear his name whispered from her lips on a silent plea.

A hanger swished, fanning the air in front of his face. He opened his eyes to find a hunk of blackened marshmallow bobbing before his eyes. "Is it done?" Marissa asked.

J.D. sighed again, tightening his fingers on Joanie's before releasing them and letting the vision go. "Yep, I believe it is."

The next afternoon, Joanie sat on the top rail of the fence that formed the arena where J.D. worked his horses, her hands cinched around the iron pipe to keep her balance, watching as J.D. put a three-year-old gelding through his paces.

Unaccustomed to the saddle and the man who sat it, the gelding danced, bucked, then tried to rear.

"Whoa, boy," J.D. murmured, his voice low and soothing. The horse backed two steps, fighting the bit and the pressure of the reins, then stopped, his powerful body quivering. After a moment, J.D. released a little of the pressure and ordered, "Walk."

Though Joanie could tell that the horse wanted to run, J.D. held him to a controlled walk and circled the arena. Four times they passed her before J.D. was satisfied the horse knew who was boss and issued a second command.

"Trot," he ordered and made a smooching sound with his lips. The horse bolted, but J.D. quickly reined him in, keeping him at a slow trot.

Around and around the arena they went, the horse's hooves kicking up a cloud of dust that hung in the air. Joanie watched, yearning to climb on the horse herself, but knew she didn't dare, not in her condition. Instead, she satisfied herself by watching J.D.

But she soon discovered that watching him was anything but satisfying. There was something sensual about the way he straddled the horse, his muscled thighs squeezed tight against the horse's sides. Biceps bulged beneath his denim work shirt as he struggled to keep the horse under control. Perspiration dampened his back and beaded his forehead while creases fanned from the corners of his narrowed eyes, his expression one of total concentration.

She'd seen him wear a similar expression that night in San Antonio when they'd first made love. But then it had been her beneath him, her hips that had felt the strength of his muscled thighs. His skin had been slick with perspiration as he'd ridden her, gently guiding her to heights she'd never known. She also remembered the afternoon on the rock, with the creek gurgling in the distance, when he'd fought to conquer a similar beast, not a horse, but an animal of sorts, she supposed, the passion that flamed like a raging forest fire between them.

A shiver coursed through her at the memory of his heated lips against her skin and she shifted uneasily on the narrow rail.

J.D. stopped the horse in front of her, swung a leg over the back of the saddle, then stepped down, his spurs jingling. Draping the reins over the rail by Joanie's foot, he teased her with a smile.

"How'd we do?"

Joanie's fingers tightened on the rail as she struggled to keep her voice light and the memories at bay.

"Great, though you might try a different bit. He doesn't seem to like that one."

J.D. chuckled and hooked a stirrup over the saddle horn. "I never met a green-broke horse that did like a bit." He uncinched the girth and let it hang while he stripped the saddle from the horse's back. He slung it over the rail beside Joanie, then draped the pad and blankets across its top to dry. He picked up a brush from a carpenter's box beneath the fence, then held it out to Joanie. "Want to brush him down?"

Joanie quickly climbed to the ground. "I thought you'd never ask." She took the brush and walked to the horse's head, letting him smell the brush and her. Threading the fingers of one hand through the straps of the horse's bridle, she made a gentle sweep down his neck.

J.D. settled a shoulder against the fence and watched.

"You know your way around horses," he said with a nod of approval.

"I should. I spent most of my life around them." She smiled, remembering, and dipped under the horse's neck to brush his other side. "Although my mother didn't approve. After having three boys, she had hoped that when she finally had a girl, she would have company in the house. But she soon learned that I preferred mucking out stalls to pushing a vacuum cleaner."

Chuckling, he pulled the brush from her hand. "A disappointment, I'm sure."

"She got over it." Joanie stepped back, inhaling deeply, loving the smell of sweat and horses and leather after so many years without it.

After putting the brush away, J.D. untied the reins and reached for Joanie's hand. Though the gesture surprised her, it pleased her more, and she fell in step beside him as he led the horse to the gate. Once they were in the pasture, he released her hand to slip off the bridle, then gave the horse a pat on the rump, signaling him that he was free. The horse took off at a gallop, tossing his head and kicking up his hind feet as he sped away to join the other horses grazing out in the pasture.

Pleasure rippled through Joanie at the sight and she stepped into the curve of J.D.'s shoulder. His arm automatically slipped around her. Together they watched the horse drop to the ground and roll, while they stood in companionable silence.

She leaned her head against his shoulder and sighed.

"Tired?" he asked, dipping his chin to look at her.

She shook her head, then gazed up at him. "No, just content."

He could see it in her eyes, in the soft smile that curved her lips, and knew that Joanie would never find life on his farm boring, a fact worth consideration. Sliding his arm to her waist, he turned her until she faced him. "I'm glad," he murmured, lifting a hand to trace her lower lip with his thumb. He felt the shudder that passed through her and all the frustrations of the past week came humming back. Drawn to her like a moth to a flame, he bent to press his lips against hers. After satisfying himself with the taste of her, he lifted his head and sighed. "I've been wanting to do that for days," he said, looking down into her leaf green eyes.

The admission surprised her. "You have?"

"Yeah. Seems like we're never alone," he said almost to himself.

"We are now."

One corner of his mouth lifted at her unexpected response. "So we are."

He bent toward her again, blocking out the sun as his lips met hers, and slipped his arms beneath her jacket to circle her waist. Opening for him, she wrapped her arms around his neck, knotting her fingers in the damp hair at his neck. Their tongues met, twined, and the earth moved beneath Joanie's feet. As sensation flooded through her, she found herself wishing for things that couldn't be. It didn't matter, though, because they were simply wishes and her secret to keep.

J.D. shifted and the rowel of his spurs jingled, the sound muffled in the ankle-deep winter grass.

In the distance, a school bus rattled to a stop.

Slowly, J.D. drew away to meet her gaze, his breathing ragged. Heat sizzled between them. "The kids are home," he murmured.

Joanie fought the sting of disappointment, then immediately felt guilty for having it as she glanced toward the road that ran in front of J.D.'s house and the bright yellow school bus with its blinking red lights. "Yeah, looks that way." She took a step back, pulling the plackets of her jacket self-consciously across her rounded middle. "I guess I'd better get back to the house. They'll want a snack."

She turned away.

"Joanie?"

She stopped and looked back. "Yes?"

He opened his mouth, wanting to ask her to stay,

or at least meet him later to finish what they had started. But he closed it before the offer slipped out, then stuck his hands deep in his pockets. It simply wouldn't be fair to either of them. He ducked his head and mumbled, "Nothing."

Joanie stood at the stove stirring a steaming pot of stew, humming softly while J.D. sat at the kitchen table, supposedly updating the farm's accounts. Bills for feed, vets and farriers were scattered across the table, yet the checkbook ledger lay forgotten beneath the pen that dangled loosely from his fingers. For some reason, he couldn't seem to keep his mind on his work.

He wanted to blame his distraction on the noise, but there wasn't any, other than the occasional scrape of Joanie's spoon against the side of the pan. With the kids at school and Lupe and Manuel in town running errands, the house was quieter than a tomb. And that was the problem, he finally admitted. The house was too quiet, a reminder that they were alone.

At that moment, Joanie chose to glance his way. When she saw him looking at her, she smiled shyly, her cheeks flushed from the heat from the stove, then turned back to her stirring. His fingers tightened convulsively on his pen.

His mouth suddenly dry, he scraped back his chair, crossed to the cupboard and pulled out a glass. He filled it with cool tap water, then gulped it down. Sighing, he set the empty glass on the counter...and realized he hadn't come close to quenching the thirst that parched his throat.

Ever since that afternoon by the creek, more than a week ago, he'd been haunted by the idea of making love to Joanie again— undressing her slowly, warming her flesh with his hands until she lay writhing beneath him, begging for him to take her. But this time, instead of satisfying only her, he would fill her with that part of him that throbbed for her. The day before, out in the pasture when they had kissed beneath the sun, had only intensified that need.

Frustrating thoughts, when he knew he had no business bedding her, not in her condition.

He stood there, silently battling his desire for her as she moved behind him, her bare feet making a slight padding sound on the tiled floor. The thought of those bare feet and the empty bed just down the hall made sweat pop out on his forehead.

You're losing it, man, he told himself. *Get a grip.* But before he could get a handle on his carnal thoughts, she was beside him, stretching to reach around him, her full breast brushing against his arm. Closing his eyes, he sucked in a sharp breath, and the scent of roses nearly brought him to his knees. He stepped back, meaning to give her room, but found himself hauling her up and into his arms instead.

Her breath came out on a surprised gasp just before his lips collided with hers. Without an ounce of hesitation, she melted against him, wrapping her arms around his neck.

And that was all the encouragement J.D. needed.

He scooped her up into his arms and staggered from the kitchen and down the hall, thinking of that empty bed and the quiet house, his mouth still ravaging hers. At the side of her bed, he stopped and slowly eased her to her feet, knowing full well that only giving her pleasure this time simply wouldn't be enough.

But could they make love without hurting her or endangering the baby? Clinging to that last thread of sanity, he lifted his hands to cup her cheeks and held her with his gaze. "I want to make love to you, but I don't want to hurt you," he told her.

She lifted her hands to cover his, her touch as soft as a butterfly's wings against his skin. "You can't hurt me, J.D.," she whispered.

"But the baby?"

A soft smile teased at her lips. "You can't hurt the baby, either," she assured him. When he continued to hesitate, she reached for the top button of his shirt. J.D. stood still as a statue as her fingers made swift work of the buttons that lined his shirt. But when her hands flattened against his chest then smoothed outward, grazing his nipples, a low moan rumbled from deep in his throat.

"Joanie, Joanie," he murmured huskily, reaching for her, "I want you so badly."

She laid her face against his bare chest, his heart like thunder beneath her cheek. "And I want you," she whispered in return.

And she did want him. All of him. She tipped her face to his, and his lips found hers again. Their fingers flew blindly, finding and discarding each other's clothes until they stood naked, their bodies pressed flush together. J.D. tore his lips from hers. "I want to see you," he said, his breathing harsh. He stepped back and pushed her to arm's length.

Heat pulsed on Joanie's cheeks, embarrassment waging a silent war with passion. Would he find her repulsive? she wondered frantically. A man like J.D. had probably been with his share of women, most of them with firm buttocks, flat stomachs and breasts that stood at attention. She was sure he'd never made love to a pregnant woman before…at least not knowingly. Would he be turned off by the changes her body had undergone?

But her fears quickly dissipated under the approval and heat she found in his gaze. He touched a tentative finger to her swollen breasts, circled the budded nipple and drew a sigh from her. She closed her eyes, blinding herself to everything but the feel of his hands on her bare flesh. His touch was gentle, almost reverent, as he took her heavy breasts within his hands and lifted. He placed a kiss on the tips of both, then released them, smoothing his hands down her stomach and gently molding the shape of the baby she carried inside.

On a sigh, he dropped to his knees, laid a cheek against her bare belly, then drifted lower until his mouth rested against the nest of hair at the juncture of her legs. Hooking his hands at the back of her thighs, he held her as he arced out his tongue, finding the most erotic spots to tease.

Joanie's breath came in ragged gasps and her knees threatened to buckle as pleasure pooled like warm molasses low in her abdomen. She tangled her hands in his hair and clung to him. He lifted his head and looked at her, his eyes almost black with heat. Slowly he rose, circling her knees with one arm, her waist with the other, and lifted her up into his arms, then onto the bed.

With a welcoming smile warming her lips, Joanie opened her arms for him.

He hesitated only slightly, then pressed a knee into

the mattress before diving over the top of her. He rolled to his back, taking Joanie with him.

The thoughtfulness in the gesture touched her because she knew he still harbored some fear that he might in some way hurt her. Smiling wickedly, she straddled him, shoving back her hair, and set out to prove to him that making love to her was as safe as a stroll through the hay meadow on a summer afternoon.

J.D. lay on his side while Joanie slept, her back to him, curled against his length. Sunshine bored through the windows, warming his face, and he felt a moment's remorse at his laziness, knowing that he had work to do out in the barn. But then Joanie shifted, snuggling even closer to him, and he draped a hand across her hip, holding her to him, and told himself he wasn't going anywhere, at least not yet. The rare pleasure of having her lying naked beside him was too tempting to resist.

He lifted himself to an elbow and caught the sheaf of hair that shadowed her face and tucked it behind her ear, wanting to fill himself with the sight of her. Still swollen from their lovemaking, her lips were slightly parted. He touched them with a tentative finger and felt the moist warmth of her breath.

Content to watch her sleep, he let his thoughts drift to their lovemaking and he remembered Joanie's hesitancy when he'd told her he wanted to look at her. He'd seen the flash of fear in her eyes and knew that she must feel self-conscious about the changes her body was undergoing. But J.D. didn't see anything in the least to be ashamed about. Her breasts were fuller, granted, and her stomach more rounded than before, but if anything, he thought her more attractive than ever.

He found himself wondering what it would be like to wake up every morning with her curled against him. The thought had surfaced more than once in the weeks that she'd been at his farm. He'd never considered taking a wife before, especially not one that came already packaged with two kids…three kids, he silently corrected and shifted his gaze to her stomach.

A baby grew there, he reminded himself. *His baby.* He smoothed his hand down her hip, then tucked it beneath her rounded stomach, testing himself to see if he felt anything, some kind of emotional tie to the child in her womb. But nothing came. As hard as he concentrated and willed it, not one blessed thing came.

Releasing a breath, he moved his hand back to her hip. A wife and kids, he thought again. A family. He and Joanie, Marissa and Shane, and another child on the way. They loved the farm, the lot of them, and would never feel the restrictions that others might. He supposed it was because Joanie had grown up on a farm much like his. Her family had raised cattle, he remembered, not horses, but the life was much the same.

He closed his eyes, letting the images, the possibilities, take shape.

But the images that came were old ones, flipping through his mind from a distance of twenty years. J.D. squeezed his eyes shut tighter, trying to blot out the painful memories, but they came anyway, slamming against his heart with an angry vengeance. Visions of broken-down fencing, sagging gates, empty barns sorely in need of paint. The weight of defeat that stooped his father's shoulders...

He rolled away from Joanie to sit on the side of the bed, the heels of his hands pressed hard against his eyes. "No," he groaned, the single word tearing at his raw throat.

"J.D.?" Joanie sat up and scooted behind him, laying a hand on his shoulder. "Honey, is something wrong?" she asked sleepily.

He jerked away from her grasp and grabbed his jeans from the pile of clothes on the floor. "No, nothing," he replied, keeping his back to her as he pulled on his pants. "I've got work to do." Snatching up his shirt and boots, he left the room.

In the loft, J.D. curled his fingers around rough twine and lifted the bale of hay. Straining at the weight, he walked to the edge and dropped it to the alleyway below. It hit the other bales he'd thrown down, then bounced away, scattering straw. He turned and grabbed another one, needing the sheer physicalness of the act to work off the anger that boiled inside him.

"You're a fool, Cawthon," he muttered under his breath. "You can't have it all. You know that." He heaved the bale over the side and immediately turned back for another.

"Hey! Watch out!" a voice called from below.

J.D. whipped back and looked over the edge to see Joanie standing below. She glared up at him from a distance of fifteen feet.

Her hands were fisted at her hips against the cotton shift he'd peeled from her only hours before. Her hair, still rumpled from their lovemaking, gleamed like warm honey in the shaft of sunlight shooting through the barn door behind her. The bale he'd just thrown lay at her feet.

"What do you want?" he grumbled.

"To talk to you," she replied.

"I've got work to do," he said, then turned to grab another bale.

Joanie perched herself on the bale of hay that had narrowly missed her and folded her arms beneath her breasts. "Fine. I can wait."

With a muffled curse, J.D. threw the last bale, aiming it at the far side of the pile and away from Joanie. She watched it slam against the others and burst from the binding, sending a spray of straw and dust blossoming into the air.

"Nice shot," she murmured dryly.

With the hay he needed on the floor below, there was nothing to keep J.D. in the loft any longer. He climbed reluctantly down the ladder, his boots scraping against the scarred wooden rungs. Once in the alleyway, he grabbed the nearest bale and carried it to a stall, dropping it in front of the gate. He whipped out a knife, sliced through the twine, then folded the blade and shoved it back in his pocket. Breaking off a section of hay, he lifted it and threw it into the empty manger.

Joanie watched in silence, her temper simmering just beneath the surface. If he thought he could ignore her, hoping that if he did so long enough she would go away, he had another think coming. She could see the anger bubbling inside him and barely held in check. It was that anger that had brought her to the barn and she wasn't leaving until she discovered its source. A woman who chose to face problems head-on, rather than skirting them, she asked, "Why are you so upset?"

J.D. stalked back to the pile of hay bales, refusing to look at her. "Like I told you, I've got work to do."

"There's always work on a farm, J.D.," she replied, refusing to let him hide behind that feeble excuse. "You're mad and I'd like to know why."

He stopped, his chest heaving beneath his sweat-dampened shirt and cut his gaze to hers. "I don't want a family," he ground out, then reached for another bale.

Joanie's heart slammed against her chest at the bitterness in his reply. So that was it, she told herself, her shoulders tensing in defense. A little sex in the afternoon and he assumed she'd start hearing wedding bells. "I don't recall asking you to take one on." She stood, her knees shaking uncontrollably. "I'll pack our things. We can leave as soon as the kids get home from school."

J.D. lifted the bale above his head and heaved it in frustration. It slammed against the stall door, rocking it back against its hinges. "I don't want you to leave," he almost yelled, wheeling on her.

"Well, what *do* you want?" she cried.

He stood, his body trembling in barely controlled rage for several heart-stopping seconds, then he dropped onto the bale and buried his face in his hands. "I don't know," he mumbled miserably, dragging his fingers through his hair. He sat there a moment, then lifted his gaze to hers.

Joanie saw the confusion in his eyes, the pain. Her anger dissolved as quickly as it had come.

"It's because we made love this afternoon, isn't it?" she asked gently.

"Yes—no." He raked his fingers through his hair again. "Damn," he muttered helplessly, "I don't know."

"Oh, J.D.," she murmured and crossed to him to place a comforting hand on his shoulder. "Can't we have even that?"

He closed his hand over hers and squeezed. "I want you," he said, the admission costing him dearly. "And I care for you. You have to know that."

"I do, J.D.," she said gently.

He tugged her hand, drawing her down beside him, then propped his elbows on his knees, flattening her hand between his palms. He kept his gaze on their joined hands. "I'm scared, Joanie."

Her brow knitted in a frown as she strained to look at his face. "Scared? Of what?"

Ashamed of his own selfishness, he lifted his shoulders then lowered them on a shuddery sigh. "My farm's important to me," he began slowly, then stopped, unsure of how to put his fears into words.

"I know that."

"And I don't want to jeopardize its success."

"I'd never ask you to," she told him.

He turned his head to look at her, and saw the truth of that in her eyes. If possible, it increased his shame.

Her smile softened. "You're a good man, J.D. An honorable one." When he opened his mouth to argue the point, she pressed a finger to his lips. "You are, or you wouldn't feel the weight of guilt so strongly."

She dropped her hand to her lap. "But I've told you, J.D., I don't want or expect anything from you. When our baby's born, I'm going home. To *my* home," she clarified, wanting to make sure he understood. "Nothing you do or say will change that."

The shame continued to eat at J.D., gnawing at his conscience far into the night. He lay in his bed, staring at the ceiling, his fingers laced across his chest. His heart thundered beneath his palms, as Joanie's words played through his mind again and again.

You're a good man, J.D. An honorable one.

He shifted uneasily against the sheet. Hell, he wasn't honorable. If he were, he'd have kept a rein on his hormones and let common sense rule. But he hadn't. Not in San Antonio. And certainly not this afternoon.

He was selfish. Selfish clear to the bone, wanting nothing more than to satisfy his lust with a woman who deserved more than a toss in the hay. And she did deserve more, he thought with another stab of guilt. More than he was willing to give.

When our baby's born, I'm going home. To my home.

The words should have brought relief, but as they played through his mind again, he bolted from the bed. He paced its length, as he raked his fingers through his already touseled hair. That was the real problem, he told himself, while his heart threatened to pound a hole in his chest.

He didn't want her to go home.

He stopped at the foot of the bed, curling his fingers around the bed's post, sure that he was suffering a heart attack. There was an ache in his chest, a numbness in his left arm. Hell, his whole body felt numb. But he wasn't having a heart attack. The cause of his pain lay sleeping in the room just down the hall.

It's because we made love this afternoon, isn't it? Can't we have even that?

A sigh shuddered through him as he bowed his head against his chest. Yes, he could give her that, but wasn't it selfishness rather than a gift, if he wanted it, too? It didn't matter, he told himself as he strode out the door and down the hall. To deny either of them would be impossible.

When he reached her room, his courage flagged, if only briefly, when he saw her sleeping form outlined in the moonlight. Then he lifted the covers and slipped into her bed. Settling himself against her back, he wrapped his arm around her, snugging it beneath her breasts.

She lifted her head, craning her neck to peer over her shoulder. "J.D.?" she asked sleepily.

"Ssshh," he soothed, smoothing a hand down her hair. "I just want to hold you," he whispered.

Sighing softly, she settled her cheek back into the dent in her pillow, then closed her hand over his and drifted back to sleep.

Chapter Eight

Fall, always slow to arrive in Central Texas, made its presence known in the third week of November, with a light frost to brighten the brown grass in the morning sun. As J.D. tramped his way to the barn with Marissa and Shane skipping along at his side, he listened to the crunch of their sneakers against the stiff grass and the pepper of questions shot his way and was somehow soothed by it all.

A man who'd spent the better part of his life alone, he realized now that he'd grown accustomed over the past two months to having the twins dog his every step...and would miss them when they were gone.

He held the barn door open while two blond heads, the same shade of honey as their mother's, bobbed beneath his arm. He could see a little of their mother in each of them. Marissa had Joanie's sparkling green eyes, her pert nose. Shane had inherited her stubborn chin, the slash of high cheekbones. A thought flashed out of nowhere. What had their father contributed?

J.D. had never given much thought to the man who'd fathered them, other than the one time he'd quizzed Joanie about whether he ever helped out, and couldn't imagine from where or why the thought had arisen. But now, suddenly, he wondered about the man, what he looked like, if the twins resembled him at all. The guy had planted seeds and transmitted his share of genes, which resulted in these two kids.

Planted seeds. The idea built, engulfing him until he focused on only one thought...the conception. Something strong and feral slowly worked its way through his body, tensing the muscles in his neck and in his jaw and squeezing its green, bony fingers around his heart. He'd never experienced the feeling before and it took him a moment to identify the strange emotion.

Jealousy.

He took a long, shaky breath and wiped his hand across his eyes, trying to block out the unwanted thoughts. They came anyway, blinding him to the familiar sights and smells in the barn. Joanie lying naked with another man, a faceless man, her legs spread for him, reaching for him, her face flushed with passion, her—

"J.D., are you coming?"

J.D. shook his head to clear the vision and saw Marissa standing in front of him, a curious look on her face.

"Yeah," he mumbled, letting the barn door close

behind him and succeeding in locking the vision on the other side. "I'm right behind you."

J.D. sat down to the first Thanksgiving dinner ever served in his house and tried to remember the last time he'd eaten the traditional holiday meal in a family setting. More than sixteen years ago, he figured. He'd spent twelve riding the circuit and had usually celebrated Thanksgiving in truck-stop cafés along the way with nothing but a bunch of cowboys for company. Their conversation was usually anything but thankful. The past four he'd spent on his farm, the day passing like any other day, with nothing but work on his menu. He'd usually choke down a dry bologna sandwich in the evening and sip beer while watching football on TV.

Nothing like the fare spread before him now. Roast turkey carved into thick, juicy slices. A bowl heaped high with corn-bread dressing. A tempting casserole of sweet potatoes topped with golden marshmallows. Green beans. Pearl onions swimming in butter. Rolls piled high in a linen-lined basket. His mouth watered at the sight.

He dragged his napkin to his lap and reached for the platter of turkey.

"Aren't we going to say what we're thankful for before we eat?" Marissa asked, her hands folded primly in her lap.

J.D. froze, his hand on the platter. He cut a glance at Joanie, who was trying her best to smother a laugh. He pulled back his hand and rubbed it against his thigh. "Yeah, I guess so. Why don't you go first?"

Marissa wiggled smugly in her chair, obviously

pleased that she got to go first. "I'm thankful for God and our country. For the Pilgrims who landed on Plymouth Rock. For my new school and my new friends. For my cat, Esmerelda. For my mama and my brother…"

The list went on and on while she named friends and relatives, some of them he'd never heard of before. His stomach rumbling, he started to yawn, then nearly choked when he heard his own name mentioned.

"And I'm thankful most for J.D. and being here on his farm." She smiled proudly at J.D., then turned her attention to Shane.

Shane ducked his head and mumbled, "I'm thankful for everything Marissa said, but most of all for the horses. Especially Windclaimer."

Marissa rolled her eyes at her brother's uninspired attempt at gratitude before turning to J.D. "It's your turn, J.D. What are you thankful for?"

J.D. couldn't have spoken a word if his life depended on it. No one in his entire life had ever said they were thankful for him. Not that he'd done anything to deserve any thanks. He'd lived his life to please himself, and to hell with everyone else. And now this little bit of nothing of a girl, who looked so much like her mother it made his heart ache, suddenly brought him to his knees with her simple words. He didn't deserve her gratitude, none of it. Yet denying it was impossible, because emotion clotted his throat, making speech impossible.

"Why don't we eat before the food gets cold?" Joanie suggested and reached for the platter of turkey.

She dragged it closer to her plate. "Marissa, pass your plate, sweetheart. Do you want white or dark meat?"

J.D.'s breath came out on a ragged sigh as plates were passed in front of him.

What had he done to deserve that kind of gratitude? he asked himself again.

J.D. sat in his recliner watching a football game while Marissa and Shane lay on the floor, a board game spread open between them. Joanie sat on the sofa, knitting needles clicking as she worked a strand of blue yarn between their tips.

"You cheated," Shane accused irritably.

"Did not," Marissa sassed back.

"If you can't play without fussing, put the game away," Joanie ordered without missing a stitch.

Both children lifted their heads to look at her, then turned back to their game, chastened. J.D. tried hard not to smile.

The doorbell sounded, its chime unfamiliar. J.D. frowned, wondering who'd use the front door. Most folks he knew came to the back. He kicked the foot of the recliner into place and rose. He peered through the front window, noting the spanking new red pickup parked in front of the house, and figured it must be some stranger who'd come to see him about purchasing a horse.

Before he could open the door all the way, Marissa and Shane were pressing at the back of his thighs, peering around him.

He dipped his head to look at them, chuckling, then turned to greet the man who stood in front of them. But before the first word of greeting passed his lips,

Marissa was tearing around him and screaming at the top of her lungs.

"Daddy! Daddy!" she cried, looping her arms around the man's legs. "You're here! You're really here!"

The man stooped and swung Marissa up into the air, then caught her against his chest. "Hey, sunshine. You better believe I'm here."

J.D. heard a sharp intake of breath and turned to find Joanie standing in the hallway behind him, her gaze frozen on the man standing on the porch.

The man turned his gaze on her, and a self-conscious smile tugged at the corner of his mouth. "Hello, Joanie."

"Hello, Josh," she murmured, then gave Shane a gentle push. "Say hello to your daddy, Shane."

Shane scuffed out onto the porch and suffered through a one-armed hug, then immediately returned to J.D.'s side, pressing his shoulder against J.D.'s hip. Without thinking, J.D. laid a hand on the boy's head. The stranger named Josh looked from the hand that covered his son's head to J.D., his gaze narrowing. J.D. kept the hand in place.

Aware of the tension that stretched between the two men and hoping to ease it, Joanie stepped closer to the doorway. "J.D., this is Josh Summers, the twins' dad. Josh, this is J. D. Cawthon."

Josh's eyes widened a bit when Joanie stepped into view, his gaze going immediately to her stomach. He shifted Marissa to one arm, his gaze going to J.D. as he extended his hand. "Glad to meet you."

J.D. hesitated a heart-stopping second before extending his own. "Same here," he muttered, though he didn't mean a word of it.

"How'd you know where to find us?" Joanie asked.

"Serena."

Joanie nodded, suspecting as much, though she knew he could have just as easily gotten the information from his parents. She'd told her in-laws about her pregnancy prior to her move to J.D.'s, and though they'd been shocked at the news, they trusted Joanie and had given her their full support as they had so many times in the past. Aware of the rocky relationship Josh maintained with his parents, she suspected he had an ulterior motive for appearing at J.D.'s so unexpectedly. His next words confirmed her suspicions.

"I was on my way to visit Mom and Dad and wondered if you'd mind if I take the twins along?"

Joanie felt her heart tighten in her chest. "For how long?"

"Just a couple of days."

Though the idea of the twins' being away from her was anything but appealing, Joanie felt it was his right. After all, he was their father and the twins needed to spend what time they could with him. "As long as you have them back by Sunday. They have school Monday."

"No problem."

Shane tipped his face up to hers, his eyes beseeching. "Do I have to, Mama?" he asked, his voice trembling.

Joanie dropped to her knees, her heart going out to her son. "It's just for a few days, Shane. And you'll get to see Mimi and Pawpaw." He hung his head.

Joanie slipped her arm around his shoulder and pulled him to her in a tight hug. "Everything'll be okay," she whispered. "I promise." And prayed that it would.

While Joanie got the kids ready, J.D. excused himself, telling Joanie he had things to do in the barn. The truth of the matter was, he didn't think he could stand watching the kids pack their things and drive away in the truck.

Yet, when he heard the truck engine roar to life, he stepped into the open doorway of the barn and watched the truck make a tight circle, then race down the lane, kicking up a long trail of dust. The last thing he saw was Shane's face, pressed to the back window, tears streaking down his cheeks.

Cursing violently, he wheeled and kicked at a bucket of feed, sending it flying across the barn floor. Why'd her ex have to come, he raged inwardly. Why today? And why did Joanie make Shane go with him when the kid obviously didn't want to leave?

He thought about that spanking new truck and the money it represented. Money Joanie and the kids could have used for more basic things like food and clothing.

"J.D.?" He turned to find Joanie standing in the doorway, her eyes red from crying, her hands pressed over her heart. He opened his arms and she ran into them. He held her while she cried, her shoulders hitching against his chest, her tears soaking the front of his shirt. She kept murmuring over and over again, "My babies. My babies."

J.D. pushed her to arm's length. "We'll go get

them,'' he said, his voice tight with anger. ''They don't have to go with him.''

Joanie hiccuped, flattening her hands against J.D.'s chest, needing his strength, but knowing he was wrong. They did have to go with him. She shook her head. ''No, it's his right. He's their father.''

''And what kind of father is he?'' he all but yelled. ''Did you see the look on Shane's face?'' he demanded, giving her a hard shake. ''He didn't want to go, but you made him.''

Her sobs increased. ''I had to,'' she cried. ''Don't you see? Shane needs to know his father, spend time with him. Some day he'll understand.''

J.D. knew she was right, but God, he couldn't forget the look on that little boy's face as he'd driven away. He pulled Joanie roughly to him, cupping the back of her head in his hand. He rocked her, needing her at that moment as much as she needed him.

''I'm sorry, Joanie,'' he murmured against her hair. ''I had no right to say those things.''

Her hands tightened against his shirt. Slowly, he realized that his anger was more than just the memory of Shane's face. It was the man. Josh Summers. He finally had a face to put on the man who'd slept with Joanie, the one who had planted the seeds that helped create Marissa and Shane. The man whose name she still carried. That vision slipped inside the barn again, the one he'd thought he'd locked on the outside earlier that day, and proceeded to burn a hole in his chest.

''Do you still love him?'' he asked, though he wasn't sure he wanted to hear her answer.

Joanie stiffened at the question, then forced herself to relax. ''No.''

"But you did?" he pressed.

"Yes, I once thought I did, long ago. But there's nothing between us now but the twins."

He felt the pressure of her rounded stomach against his groin and thought of the baby that grew there. His baby. "Is that all there is between us? The baby we share?"

A sigh shuddered through Joanie. "No," she whispered. "At least not for me." She stepped from his embrace, knowing that it was time to share her feelings with him. "I love you, J.D. I have for as long as I can remember."

Her words stunned him. "But you married Josh Summers," he said, his mind spinning crazily.

"Yes, I did. But you were my first true love. I was thirteen the first time I saw you. Eighteen the last when I watched you win the title of National Champion. The five years in between I mooned over you like a lovesick teenager. Do you remember kissing me?" she asked softly. When his brow knitted into a puzzled frown, she said, "I do. It was the night you won the title for the first time. I was behind the chutes waiting for George when you came through the gate. You grabbed me up and kissed me. I've never forgotten that kiss."

That she remembered and he didn't shamed him. Oh, he remembered Joanie all right. She, as well as her parents, had attended every rodeo her brother George had ever ridden in. Over the years, he'd envied George the support, the love that he'd received from his family. His own parents had never traveled to watch him ride. The only support he'd ever received had been in the form of the entry fee he'd needed for the first couple of rides and it had been his mother, in secret, who'd pressed those hard-earned dollars into his hand.

Yes, he remembered Joanie. But he'd never seen her as anyone other than George Hill's kid sister. And as far as the kiss was concerned, he had no memory of that at all.

Joanie laughed softly at his look of distress. "You were higher than a kite, flying on adrenaline."

J.D. just shook his head.

"When I saw you again in San Antonio, it was as if I'd been given a second chance. I couldn't have said no to you that night even if I'd wanted to. Making love with you was something I'd dreamed of most of my life."

J.D. just stared, unable to think of a thing to say.

"I've frightened you, haven't I?" She reached for his hands and clasped them in hers. "I didn't mean to. My feelings for you don't change anything, J.D. They are mine. I don't expect you to share them."

J.D. heard the front door burst open, then the sound of a truck driving away. He bumped into Joanie in the hallway and ended up struggling with her as they both tried to shoulder their way through the narrow doorway at the same time.

When they made it to the entry hall, they found Marissa and Shane standing there, their suitcases at their feet.

"Where's your dad?" Joanie asked, unable to hide her surprise at seeing the twins again so soon. They'd been gone less than twenty-four hours.

Shane ducked his head, the tips of his ears turning

a bright red. Marissa sank onto the top of her suitcase, dropping her chin to her palms and her elbows to her knees. "Daddy and Pawpaw had a fight," she said with a huff.

"A fight!" Joanie echoed. "About what?"

"I'm not sure. But I heard Pawpaw yelling at Daddy, asking him if he was ever going to grow up."

Joanie bit back a smile. The argument was a familiar one she'd heard herself over the years. "And that made your daddy mad?"

"I'll say," Marissa said, standing and picking up her suitcase. "Before you could say spit, Daddy was throwing our stuff in our suitcases and loading us into his truck." She headed down the hall for her room, the ugly scene for her already forgotten. "Where is Esmerelda?" she called over her shoulder.

"Out in the barn, I think." Joanie looked at Shane. "You okay?" she asked softly. He never lifted his head to look at her, just nodded, grabbed the straps of his bag and followed Marissa down the hall.

Joanie folded her arms beneath her breasts and watched her son go, her heart going out to him.

J.D. laid a hand on her shoulder. "He'll be okay," he assured her.

Joanie covered his hand with her own. "I hope so," she replied, sighing. "I certainly hope so."

J.D. stepped into the doorway of the twins' bedroom and found Shane lying on his bed, his chin propped on his palms, staring out the window. The room looked nothing like it had before the kids had arrived. Once an empty shell, the room now was filled with their twin beds, matching chests they'd brought with them and a bookshelf that held their toys and games. They'd definitely left their stamp on the room, making it their own.

Shane's duffel bag lay open at the foot of his bed. The sleeve of a denim jacket swung like the trunk of an elephant from its zippered opening keeping time with the silent sobs that shook the boy's shoulders.

J.D. stepped inside and pulled the jacket from the bag and folded it in half. "What are you looking at?" he asked.

Shane tensed, then quickly dragged his wrists beneath his eyes to hide his tears. "Nothing. Just looking."

"I was thinking about going for a ride. Want to come along?"

Shane rolled to his side to peer at J.D. Though tears still gleamed in his eyes, J.D. saw his look of hopeful expectancy and wondered why he'd never offered to let the boy ride before.

"Could I?"

J.D. tossed him the jacket. "Sure. Put on your jacket and tell your mother where you're going. I'll be out in the barn saddling our horses."

He turned away, but Shane's soft request stopped him.

"J.D.?"

"Yeah?"

"Could I ride Windclaimer?"

J.D. smiled ruefully, remembering the boy's Thanksgiving prayer. "You bet."

J.D. tightened the cinch and unhooked the stirrup, letting it settle into place at Windclaimer's side. Shane stood at the horse's nose, his face wreathed in a bright smile.

"Have you ever ridden before?" J.D. asked.

"Once. When I was little. We were visiting my grandparents in Wyoming and Uncle George let me ride his horse, Dandy."

J.D. snorted. "George still has that old bag of bones?"

"You know my uncle George?" Shane asked, his eyes round in surprise.

"Used to ride the circuit with him."

"Wow! You're a bronc rider, too?"

"Was. I don't ride broncs anymore, at least not professionally."

"How come?"

J.D. caught the boy under the armpits and swung him up into the saddle. "Don't need to. I got what I want from riding."

Though Shane looked disappointed to discover that J.D. no longer rode broncs, he said earnestly, "I'll bet you were the best."

J.D. swung up onto his own horse and wound Windclaimer's lead rope around his saddle horn. "I won my share." He grinned at the boy. "Ready for a ride, cowboy?"

Shane grabbed the reins with one hand, braced his other on the saddle horn and grinned. "You betcha."

With a touch of his spurs, J.D. headed his horse for the north pasture with Windclaimer following a step behind. They rode in silence while J.D. tried to think of some way to bring up the boy's father without upsetting the child again. He had to make sure the man's callous behavior hadn't done any permanent damage to the boy. "Too bad about your dad having to cut short his trip," he finally said, glancing back over his shoulder.

His comment won a frown. "I didn't mind," Shane said. "I'd rather be here with you."

Not with his mother, as J.D. had expected him to say, but with him. The idea that the boy would want to be with him touched J.D., but also troubled him. He didn't want the boy thinking of him as a replacement for his father. He'd disappoint him, as surely as his old man had. "But he's your dad."

"No, he's not," Shane replied quickly, his voice filled with anger. "If he were, he'd live with us like other kids' dads do."

J.D. felt a knife stab through his chest. Would his own child feel that way? he wondered. Would he grow to resent him as Shane did his father because he wasn't there? J.D. let a sigh ease from him. It seemed that in trying to pull Shane out of one of life's many ditches, he'd fallen into one himself.

"But he's still your dad whether he lives with you or not," J.D. said firmly. "Nothing will change that."

Shane didn't reply, but looked at J.D., his eyes narrowed in doubt.

J.D. debated whether to force the issue, then decided some things were best left alone. "Want to try a trot?"

Shane tightened his legs around the horse's sides, his dark mood disappearing instantly. "Yeah, sure!!"

With a touch of his heels, J.D. spurred his horse into a trot, forcing Windclaimer into one, as well. Shane bobbed up and down on the saddle, laughing, his blue mood gone.

Unfortunately, J.D.'s mood wasn't as easy to escape.

J.D. stuck his head into the kitchen. "I'm headed for town. Do you need anything?"

Joanie set the last plate into the dish drainer and turned, drying her hands on the apron. With her stomach now as round as a basketball, the scrap of cloth barely covered it. "Would you mind if I ride along? I need to do some Christmas shopping."

"No problem. As long as you don't mind waiting while I pick up some feed at the feed store."

"I don't mind." She headed for the refrigerator. "Just give me a second to put out some meat to thaw for lunch."

"Why don't we grab a bite to eat in town?"

She laughed, letting the refrigerator door close as quickly as she'd opened it. "You don't have to ask me twice."

"It's a date, then."

A date? She and J.D. had never had a *real* date. They lived together. But a date? In spite of herself, Joanie felt a bubble of excitement at the possibility. "Do I have time to freshen up?"

"Take all the time you need. I'll be in the barn when you're ready."

As soon as the back door closed behind J.D., Joanie stripped the apron from her waist and ran to her room. She hurried to her closet, pulled out a maternity sweater of the same shade of green as her eyes and a pair of stirrup pants of the same color. Wiggling out of her dress, she quickly pulled on the pants, easing the elastic panel across her swollen stomach. After pulling the sweater over her head, she dug a pair of flats out of the closet and squeezed her swollen feet into them, grumbling her dissatisfaction at the latest symptom of pregnancy.

Once the shoes were on, she picked up her brush and ran it through her hair. A swipe of lipstick and a flick of the mascara wand followed.

Stepping back from the dresser, she assessed her reflection in the mirror. The light dimmed in her eyes and her smile slowly melted away. She placed a hand on her rounded middle. The fingers she spread there were as swollen as her feet.

Tears glimmered in her eyes. She wanted so desperately to look pretty for J.D. She was sick to death of feeling fat and ugly. She sank onto the bed and let the tears flow.

J.D. found her there.

He frowned as he eased into the room. "Joanie? Honey, is something wrong?"

She sniffed and shifted on the bed, angling her body away from him. "No, nothing. Go on without me. I'll do my shopping later."

J.D. sat behind her, placing a hand on her shoulder. "I'm not going anywhere until you tell me why you're crying."

"It's nothing, really," she said. "I just have too much to do to be running off to town."

J.D. rose, then hunkered down in front of her. He put a finger beneath her chin, forcing her head up. "As I remember you telling me, there's always work to be done. What's the real reason?"

Her eyes filled with tears again and her chin quivered. She fanned her hands out in front of his face.

"Just look," she said on a hiccup. "My fingers are as fat as sausages."

Before he could even focus on her swollen fingers, she snatched them back, digging her hands into the mattress as she kicked up her feet. "And look at these," she cried. "I'm fat and ugly and I'm sick of it."

J.D. would've laughed, but he could see that that was what she really thought. "Oh, Joanie, honey. You're not fat, you're pregnant. And the most beautiful pregnant woman I've ever laid eyes on," he added, gathering her into his arms for a hug.

"I know I'm pregnant," she wailed, her tears soaking the front of his shirt. "And I don't want to be pregnant anymore."

J.D. couldn't stifle the chuckle this time. It rumbled through him before he could stop it.

Joanie shoved at his chest, pushing herself from his arms. "It's not funny," she cried, swiping angrily at her tears. "I feel like I've been pregnant forever, like I'm going to be this way the rest of my life."

"You're not. You know that. You've only got about a month to go."

"A month! Easy for you to say. You're not waddling around like a duck with your feet squeezed into shoes that pinch your feet and your fingers so swollen you can't wear any rings."

It was true. He didn't suffer all the discomforts of pregnancy. But he knew how to make them a little more tolerable. He stood and crossed to her closet, picking up the house slippers she'd kicked off when she'd changed clothes. He returned to the bed and knelt in front of her. He eased the tight shoes off her feet, pressed a kiss to the angry red marks that they'd left, then slipped on the slippers. "Better?" he asked, looking up at her.

Joanie's fingers, enlarged as they were, were pressed to her lips. She nodded.

Hunkering back on his heels, he gently pulled her hands from her mouth. He kissed each finger in turn. "We'll get your rings sized while we're in town, or, if you want, we'll buy you some new ones."

Joanie sat with her mouth open, staring at him as if he'd just offered to buy her New York City, then threw her arms around his neck and buried her face in his shoulder. "Oh, J.D.," she sobbed, "that's the sweetest thing anyone has ever done for me."

Joanie fingered the tooled leather strap, remembering how much Shane had admired J.D.'s and wishing she could buy him one and have his name carved on its back. She could almost see his face, his whoop of excitement when he opened it on Christmas morning.

She dropped the belt, letting it fall back into place with the others on the rack, silently scolding herself for the frivolous thought. She couldn't afford to buy her children luxuries for Christmas, not when they needed so many essentials. Like a new jacket, she told herself and made herself cross to a rack nearby. Shane had grown so much over the past few months that the sleeves of his denim jacket were a good two inches too short for his arms.

She flipped through the jackets until she found one in Shane's size. Sighing, she pulled it from the rack and turned, bumping her nose against J.D.'s chest.

J.D. took the jacket from her and offered her his arm. "You about ready?" he asked.

She slipped her arm through his and nodded. "Yes, as ready as I'll ever be. How about you?"

"They're loading the feed now." He walked with her to the register at the front, where Joanie had several other items waiting.

The salesclerk glanced at Joanie's slippers and chuckled. "Feet swollen, huh?"

Joanie looked at J.D. and they both laughed. "You could say that."

"Mine always did, too, when I was pregnant. When are you due?"

Joanie took the jacket from J.D. and added it to the pile of her other purchases. "January."

"It'll be here before you know it," she said with a wink. "Are you ready to check out?"

"Yes, I am."

J.D. leaned over to whisper in her ear. "I'm going to run to the rest room. I'll meet you at the truck."

Her attention on the items the salesclerk was totaling, Joanie murmured her agreement.

J.D. strode toward the rest rooms, then glanced back over his shoulder. When he was sure Joanie wasn't looking, he darted between two racks of men's shirts, then wove his way to the belts.

"Could I help you, sir?" a young woman asked.

"Yeah. I want one of these." He pulled the belt he'd seen Joanie looking at and passed it to the clerk. He stole another glance over his shoulder to the front of the store, then turned back to the young woman. "Would you put the name Shane on the back?"

The woman smiled. "I'd be happy to."

* * *

J.D. flopped the tree down in front of the den window, then stepped back, holding it in place. "Is it straight?" he asked.

Joanie frowned at the full cedar tree, her elbow propped on her stomach and her chin in her hand. "It's leaning just a little to the left," she said, then waited while J.D. made the necessary adjustments. "A little bit more. A little bit more. Perfect!" she cried, folding her hands prayer-like beneath her chin.

J.D. stood, dusting needles from his knees. "Now what?"

"We need decorations."

J.D.'s hands froze on his thighs in mid-swipe. "If you're thinking I have Christmas decorations, you're going to be disappointed, 'cause I don't." He waved a hand at the tree. "In fact, this is the first Christmas tree that's ever shed a needle in this room."

Learning that he'd never celebrated Christmas made an unexpected lump rise in Joanie's throat. "Don't worry," she told him. "We can make our own. It'll be more fun." She frowned again. "But lights might be a problem."

J.D. thought for a minute, eyeing the tree. "I've got a couple of strings of lights that I used for a barbecue last year when I entertained some horse buyers. Think that would do?"

"They'll be perfect."

While Joanie and Marissa gathered paper, scissors and glue, J.D. and Shane made a fast trip to the barn to search for the lights. When they returned, Marissa and Joanie were sitting on the floor in front of the tree, cutting stars from foil paper.

Marissa held up a lopsided star for J.D.'s inspection. "Look what I made," she called out, obviously pleased with herself.

J.D. hauled her up, star and all. "Why, that's the prettiest star I've ever seen. I believe it deserves top billing, don't you?"

Marissa giggled. "What's top billing?"

J.D. pointed. "The top of the tree." He lifted her, letting her nestle the star against the highest branch, then set her back down. He lifted his nose, sniffing. "Do I smell popcorn?"

"You certainly do and you can't have any," Joanie warned. "It's for the tree. I'm going to thread it through a string later after it cools." She nodded toward the tree. "You better start placing the lights. Marissa and I'll have the decorations made soon."

And so their evening went, with only a break for dinner to interrupt the decorating of the first Christmas tree that had ever graced J.D.'s den.

When all the decorations were in place, J.D. plugged in the string of lights and the little bulbs popped on, glimmering through the tree's branches like stars twinkling in the night. Marissa and Shane cheered, then made a wild dive for J.D.'s recliner when he started to sit down.

"Hey! What's this?" he demanded to know, twisting around to look behind him.

"We want to sit in your chair while we watch 'The Grinch Who Stole Christmas.' Can we, please?"

With their shoulders snugged so close together, they looked like two peas in a pod and as impish as two little monsters. J.D. couldn't have denied them the

pleasure even if he'd wanted to. "I suppose, but just this once," he warned playfully.

He detoured to the sofa, where Joanie was stretched out, painstakingly threading puffs of white popcorn through a needle, her feet crossed on the cushion. Lifting her feet, he sat down, then settled her feet on his lap. Unconsciously, he began to massage the arch of one swollen foot as he turned his gaze on the television.

"Ooohh!"

J.D. jumped at the unexpected groan. "What's wrong? Did you prick your finger?"

"No. The baby just kicked." Joanie set aside the bowl of popcorn and the string. She scooted across the sofa until she was sitting beside J.D. She took his hand and pressed it beneath hers on her stomach.

He sat a moment, still as a mouse. "I don't feel anything."

"Ssshh. Be patient."

Then he felt it, a solid thump against his hand. He jerked his hand back, balling it into a fist in the air. He gulped, his Adam's apple bobbing as he stared at her stomach.

Joanie laughed softly. "Strong little son of a gun, isn't he?"

He jerked his gaze to hers. "He?" he asked, thinking she knew something he didn't.

"He, she, whichever." Her eyes rounded and she grabbed his hand, pulling it back to her stomach. "He's turning over," she whispered in excitement.

J.D.'s hand rose on Joanie's stomach as a hump...a head, maybe a butt...rolled beneath his hand. He jerked his hand back and bolted to his feet, sure that he was going to lose his supper right then and there. He needed air and fast.

Joanie looked up at him, puzzled by his behavior. "J.D.? What's wrong?"

"I need—" He gulped once, then tried again. "I need to check on the horses."

Shane was shooting out of the chair. "I'll go with you."

"No!" J.D. snapped, then forced himself to calm down when he saw the hurt in Shane's eyes. "No," he said more gently. "Watch your movie. I won't be gone long."

Chapter Nine

J.D. stumbled to the barn, his chest heaving. Once inside, he pulled the door shut behind him and fell back against it.

"Jesus," he whispered, his voice cracking on the single word. He slid down the door, splinters tearing at his shirt, his legs unable to support him any longer. He covered his face with his hands.

A baby. *His* baby. For the first time in the eight plus months Joanie had carried it, the baby, the one whose existence he'd silently denied, suddenly seemed real to him. He lifted his hands to stare at them. He'd felt it, he told himself. Felt the shape of its foot when it had kicked. Felt the curve of its body when it turned over beneath his hands. Felt the life stretching Joanie's already-taut skin. A life he'd had a part in creating. A baby. *His* baby. The wonder of it made a cold sweat break out on his forehead.

He dragged his arm across his eyes, wiping with his shirtsleeve at the moisture that had gathered there. Never in his life had he experienced anything so humbling...or so terrifying.

J. D. Cawthon, a man who'd chosen a horse farm over a family, was going to be a father.

In the stall ahead of him, a horse lifted her head over the low door and nickered, a cloud of vapor forming before her nostrils in the cold. A shiver of fear worked its way down his spine at the sight of the horse and he stared until his vision blurred. The walls of the barn slowly closed in on him. His chest tightened and he gulped, trying to find enough air.

In the misty vapor that still hung in front of the horse's head, he could see his farm as if projected through time-lapse photography. The walls of his barns crumbling slowly until there was nothing left of the proud structures but rotted wood. Fence posts broken or fallen, the slick wire sagging and twisted with choking weeds. The plush pastureland he'd worked so hard to clear overtaken by scrub brush and cedar.

He leaped to his feet, pressing his hands against his temples to keep the nightmares at bay. He had to get away, he told himself, looking wildly around for a means of escape, sure that if he didn't, he'd go crazy. He wasn't ready for this, not yet. He didn't know how to be a father. Wasn't willing to take on the responsibility. He had his farm. His farm was all he'd ever needed, all he'd ever understood.

J.D. drove through the night, not even aware of the direction he was heading. He simply drove, putting distance between himself and his farm…and the family waiting for him there. When the sun spilled over the horizon, he saw the road sign for Amarillo. Without realizing his destination, he'd come home. Home to the place where the nightmares had started. Where his desire for a farm of his own had begun.

His heart thundering in his chest, he made the turn onto the hard-packed dirt road that led to his parents' home, wondering what had brought him there. He hadn't been home in almost sixteen years. He'd had no desire to see his mother's misery, the defeat that weighed so heavily on his father's shoulders, and no wish to confront his own feelings of guilt that he was part of the reason for his father's failure.

He stopped his truck in front of the frame farmhouse and stepped out, letting the dust settle around him. The place looked even worse than he remembered it. One of the porch posts leaned decidedly to the left, and the screen door sagged on its hinges. A matted dog slunk out from under the porch and headed toward him, his tail tucked between his legs.

J.D. placed a hand on the dog's head and simply stared, shocked by the desolation of what was once home to him. Paint had peeled from the exterior walls leaving scablike scars to mar the white-painted structure. Loose shingles flapped in the cold wind. He let his gaze drift beyond the house to the barns. Even from this distance, he could see that they were empty. A shiver coursed through him and he blamed it on the cold rather than on the conflicting emotions that warred within him. Reaching inside the truck, he hooked a finger in his coat, then shrugged it on.

Knowing his parents were still asleep, he strode toward the cluster of outbuildings, stuffing his hands deep into his jeans pockets. Each step he took drew him nearer and nearer the nightmares from his past...and the reality of what his own dreams might turn into. Bolstering himself with a deep breath, he stepped inside. The sun hadn't risen high enough to offer much light. The barn still lay in shadows. Cobwebs hung from every corner, draped every post, painting everything a dull, depressing gray. Stall doors gaped open on broken or rusting hinges and mildewed hay lay in tight, forgotten clumps in the mangers. Tucked in the corner against the far wall, a faded sign read Horses For Sale.

J.D. hauled in another deep breath and nearly choked on the musty smell of decay. Rubbing a trembling hand across his mouth, he wheeled and headed for the barn door. Once outside in the fresh air again, he made for the gate and the pastures beyond. He walked through the frost-stiffened grass, remembering the hours he and his brothers had spent clearing the land. Summers spent on tractors, raking and baling hay, bone-chilling winters spent chipping ice from water troughs and throwing hay and filling portable mangers with grain for the horses that had once grazed there. Hours upon hours spent in the corral breaking horses for sale. Lost. All of it lost.

Why, he asked himself in bewilderment, had his father let nature reclaim the land they'd worked so hard to improve? Why, when all the children were gone, the ones his father had claimed had kept him broke, had his old man allowed the farm to fall into ruin?

Because it was he and his brothers who had kept

the place alive. He stopped suddenly as the thought formed. It was true, he realized. It was his and his brothers' work that had kept the place afloat. Without them, his father had failed.

Without realizing he'd retraced his steps, he found himself once again in front of the house. As he neared the front porch, the screen door slapped back on its hinges and his father stepped out, shrugging suspenders over a thermal shirt.

He squinted through the early morning light. "J.D.? That you, son?" he asked in surprise.

J.D. stopped, staring at the withered and stooped man in front of him. The years hadn't been kind. A day's worth of whiskers grayed the man's jaws; his hair still tousled from sleep, shot in wild white tufts straight from his scalp.

He wanted to hate the man who stood there, the man who had cut him to the bone as a teenager with his accusations, the man who had doled out guilt instead of love. But all he felt was a tremendous sadness.

J.D. let his breath out on a shuddery sigh. "Yeah, it's me." He took the few steps that led to the porch with a calmness that defied the trembling in his knees. He clasped his father's hand in his, squeezing sixteen years' worth of greetings into one.

His father ended the brief contact by pulling his hand away.

"What brings you our way?" he asked gruffly.

"Just passing through. Thought I'd stop in and say hello."

"Your mother'll be glad to see you." Never his father, only his mother. J.D. felt the sting of that response as his father pulled open the door and held it, waiting for J.D. to pass through. "Come on inside out of the cold, son."

J.D. stepped through the front door and straight into his past. The warmth of gas space heaters, freshly lit, slowly worked its way to penetrate the chill that surrounded his heart. The interior of the house hadn't changed in the sixteen years since he'd seen it last. On the floor beneath his feet stretched the same braided oval rug he'd wrestled on with his brothers when they'd been kids. The same granny-square afghan stretched across the back of the faded couch. A floor lamp stood between the couch and his father's recliner, wearing its original lamp shade, the plastic wrapping his mother had never removed, brittle and yellow with age over the lamp's soft glow.

The house was brutally clean. Not a speck of dust in sight. It had always been so. The house was his mother's domain as much as the land that surrounded it was his father's. Though she'd had little to work with, she'd always taken pride in her housekeeping and her cooking, the only two things she'd been allowed any control over.

As if his thoughts had drawn her, his mother stepped through the door that opened to his parents' bedroom, hastily pushing buttons on her house dress through their holes.

"J.D.!" Her hands flew to her lips when she saw him and tears dampened her eyes. He opened his arms and she rushed into them, hugging her youngest child to her breast. She pushed away to hold him at arm's length. "Let me look at you," she said, sniffing back tears. "You're too skinny," she scolded gently, though he knew he'd put on a good twenty pounds since she'd seen him last.

J.D. chuckled to hide his emotions and patted his stomach. "A little of your biscuits and sausage gravy ought to rectify that."

She caught him by the hand and tugged him behind her. "What am I thinking! You're hungry, of course. Come and talk to me while I start the coffee."

Once she'd seated him at the table, she scurried around the kitchen, throwing grounds into the ancient percolator and pulling out the makings for biscuits. Within minutes, the familiar smells of breakfast cooking filled the old farmhouse kitchen.

After setting a cup of steaming coffee in front of first her husband, then her son, she turned to the stove and flipped thick slabs of sausage, then moved on to the counter and started rolling out dough. "How's your farm doing?" she asked.

"Fine. Better than fine, really." J.D. took a careful sip, grateful for the kick of caffeine after a night without any sleep. "I have twenty brood mares and three studs, plus I'm working on breaking ten geldings. They'll be ready for sale in the spring."

She stole a glance over her shoulder and smiled. "I'm proud of you, son."

His father didn't seem to share her pride. He made a huffing sound and scowled. "I imagine you've got the time and the money to spend on building a spread, being as you don't have a family to support. I can remember the day when my barns were full and people lined up with money in their hands, hankering to pay my stud fees."

The flare of temper came out of nowhere and J.D. returned sharply, "And when was that?"

His comment seemed to startle his father. No one, including J.D., had ever had the nerve to question him before. The man blustered, "Never you mind. I had my dreams, too."

But J.D. refused to let the old argument die. "We're all gone now, Dad. So who are you blaming things on now?"

He heard his mother's sharp intake of breath and glanced her way. The stricken look on her face silenced him when nothing else could.

"That's enough, the both of you," she said, her face mottled with red. She turned away, then pushed a cutter through the dough and laid the creamy white circles in a pie pan, her movements a study in self-control. When she spoke, her voice was calm again, her tone conversational as if the angry exchange had never taken place. "I don't suppose you've settled down enough to take a wife?"

J.D.'s anger was still there, lying just beneath the surface, and he struggled, for his mother's sake, to keep it there. But her question drew a whole new batch of emotions to coat the anger. He rubbed a finger around the ceramic rim of the coffee cup, his thoughts deep and unsettling. "No, but I might be considering taking one before long, if I can convince her to say yes."

If possible, his announcement shocked J.D. as much as it did his mother. He didn't know when the idea had struck him. When he'd left his farm, he'd been on the run, needing to put as much distance as possible between himself and the family that threatened the fulfillment of his dreams. Maybe it had happened in the long, solitary hours of driving or maybe only moments ago when he'd realized as a man what he'd never understood as a boy—that he and his brothers and sisters weren't the cause of his father's failure. It was his father's own shortcomings that had held him back.

His mother spun, her hands dusted with flour. "Really?"

J.D. ducked his head, centering his gaze on his cup of coffee. "Yeah." He stared a minute, debating whether he should tell them everything. After all, they had a right to know he was about to make them grandparents again. He slid down in his chair, digging his heels into the worn linoleum as he crossed his boots at the ankle. "As a matter of fact," he said, struggling to keep his voice level, "if I don't convince her pretty quick, I might be a daddy before I'm a husband."

His mother's eyes grew as round as the biscuit she held in her hand. "A daddy?" she repeated in surprise.

"Yeah." He snorted, shaking his head. "Pretty hard to grasp, even for me."

Once breakfast was over, J.D. couldn't wait to get back in his truck and headed for home. He needed to see Joanie, hold her...but most of all he needed to convince her to marry him.

He wheeled into a gas station, leaped from his truck and headed for a phone booth, digging a quarter from his pocket. Feeding it into the slot, he punched in his own number, his fingers fumbling in the cold. Joanie answered on the third ring.

"Hello."

Her voice wrapped itself around him like a thick

winter coat, warming him all the way to his soul. He sagged against the glass door of the phone booth. In the background, he could hear Marissa and Shane, their voices raised in excitement and the sound of paper tearing. Christmas morning. They would be opening their presents about now.

"Joanie, it's me, J.D."

There was a pause, a long one in which J.D. found himself holding his breath. When she finally spoke, her voice was cool. "Where are you?"

"Just outside Amarillo. I'm on my way home. It's about a ten-hour drive from here. Will you wait up for me?"

Another pause, this one even longer than the last.

"Yes, I'll wait up."

"Joanie—" He stopped, unsure what to say. How could he explain the changes he'd undergone, changes that would affect Joanie and her kids, as well. He said instead, "Merry Christmas," deciding that what was in his heart would be better said in person.

"Merry Christmas to you, too, J.D." Then the line went dead. He held the receiver a moment, clinging to that last contact, then slammed it back on the hook and ran for his truck.

It was pushing midnight when he drove his dust-covered pickup past the front of his house. Christmas lights from the tree blinked at the den window, but otherwise the house was pitch-black. He parked his truck by the side door and jumped out. Pushing open the back door, he flipped on the kitchen light and tossed his keys to the counter. After dragging off his hat, he hooked it on the peg by the door.

"Joanie?" he called softly. When she didn't answer, he headed for the den. He found her there, curled into a ball on the sofa, her knitting lying forgotten near her feet. He crossed to her, his heart lodged tight in his throat.

He knelt beside the sofa, lifting the tendrils of hair that shadowed her face and tucked them behind her ear. Silvery light from the Christmas tree gave her skin an angelic glow. God, how he loved this woman, he thought as he stared at her. Why he hadn't realized it before now, he didn't know.

"Joanie?" he urged, laying a hand against her cheek. "Wake up, sweetheart, I'm home."

Stretching out her legs, she mewed softly and slowly blinked open her eyes. When she finally focused on him, she reared back away from his touch. "What time is it?" she asked, hastily pushing herself to a sitting position.

J.D. slowly withdrew a hand that suddenly rested on nothing but air. This wasn't the welcome he'd hoped for, dreamed of, during the long drive back home. "Almost midnight."

"You made good time."

He grinned to hide his uneasiness. "I was in a hurry."

"You left in one, too."

The accusation in her voice was unmistakable. "Yeah, I did."

"Where'd you go?"

"To my parents."

"Your parents?" she asked, looking at him in surprise. "Why?"

Joanie never seemed to ask the easy questions. He

shrugged, then shoved aside the knitting to clear a spot for himself on the sofa beside her. "I needed to get away for a while."

"Run away, you mean."

The bitterness in her tone caught him off guard, but the accusation didn't surprise him at all. He knew he deserved it. "Yeah, I was running all right. You pretty much scared the hell out of me."

"Me!" she cried defensively, whipping her head around to stare at him. "What did I do?"

"Well, not you exactly." He reached over to lay a hand on her stomach. "This little kicker did." Joanie angrily brushed his hand from her stomach.

That she would deny him even that slight contact cut him to the quick. He let out a sigh. "You're mad, aren't you?"

"You might have said something before you left," she said crossly. She turned to glare at him. "Why *did* you leave?"

"To think."

She let out a huff. "You had to drive all the way to Amarillo to think?"

"Well, that wasn't my destination. That's just where I ended up."

She tossed her head and tipped up her chin. "And what was so all-fired important that you had to drive all the way to Amarillo to think about?"

"You. Us. The baby."

By the tightening of her jaw, he could see that she didn't believe him. "It's true. From the beginning, from the time you told me you were pregnant until last night when you put my hand on your stomach and I felt the baby move, that critter's been hard for me

to believe in. I knew it existed, mind you," he added
to smooth her ruffled feathers, "but somehow it never
seemed quite real." He shook his head when she refused to look at him. "You don't seem to realize.
You've been carrying it around inside you, experienc-
ing its growth. I haven't had that advantage."

She snorted, crossing her arms in the narrow space
that remained between her breasts and the basketball
that lay beneath it. "Oh, it's an advantage all right."

J.D. scooted closer and was relieved when she
didn't move away. "It is an advantage. You already
know this baby. You've felt it kick, soothed it when
it was restless, nurtured it with your own blood. I
haven't had that privilege."

Though she fought it, Joanie found herself soften-
ing. But she managed to stop just short of feeling sorry
for him. "So you felt the baby move and suddenly
paternity was a reality. Was that the reason you ran?"

"No, not totally." He blew out a breath, knowing
this part was going to be the most difficult to explain.
"I've told you how much my farm means to me and
how I feared that the responsibilities of a family would
somehow rob me of that dream."

Joanie heaved an exasperated breath. "J.D., we've
discussed this. And I've already told you—"

He silenced her with a touch of his finger to her
lips. "I know what you've said. But I'd appreciate it
if you'd hear me out." He dragged his fingers from
her lips and wished like hell he could replace them
with his lips. But he had some explaining to do before
he'd chance that. "Those fears aren't something that
I imagined. They were real to me. In fact, I lived them
every day. They were all but inbred in me.

"I grew up on a ranch much like the one I've built here. My father raised quarter horses...or at least he tried to. He never had much luck, though, at least not of the good variety. We lived day-to-day, never sure if there would be money enough to meet the bills. Daddy always blamed our troubles on us kids, claiming that keeping us clothed and fed was what kept him from turning the ranch into a profitable one. All of us worked. My sisters around the house, my brothers and I out on the farm. I was driving a tractor, baling hay by the time I was nine. Broke my first horse when I was ten. But no matter how much we helped out, it was never enough.

"Dad had one good stud. Stormy was his name. He could have made a good living off him alone. But every time someone showed an interest in breeding their mare to him, my dad would name an exorbitant price for Stormy's services and scare the customers off."

He shook his head at the memory. "When I was older, I argued with him, tried to talk him into naming a fairer price, but he refused to listen to reason, claiming that Stormy was worth every penny of the price he demanded. I guess it was about then, when I was fifteen or so, that I started dreaming of having a place of my own, a place where I could be boss.

"I'd been riding broncs for a couple of years by then, small-time rodeos mostly, and I saw that as my chance to earn the seed money I'd need for a start. It took a lot of years of chasing highways, of following the circuit to the next rodeo, the next eight-second ride. But I finally did it. I had enough money for a stake."

He chuckled. "But I guess I'd heard my dad's sermon preached one too many times, because I was convinced that I had to do it alone without the encumbrance of a family." He swiveled on the sofa until he faced Joanie. "Until you came along."

Joanie dipped her chin, plucking at the ties of her robe, not wanting to read anything into the conversation that wasn't there. "J.D., this isn't necessary. I—"

"No, it is, because when I went home, I saw that all these years I was wrong...*he* was wrong. There's no one there any more, Joanie, no one for him to support except my mother, and the place is falling down around him. I know now *he* was the reason for his farm's failure, not me, not his family."

Joanie shook her head as if nothing he was saying was making any sense...or worse, any difference.

He took her hand in his, desperate to make her understand. "Don't you see, Joanie?" he said, squeezing her hand between his. "My fears were all for nothing. I'm not like my father. I *know* I can make a success out of this place, no matter what. We can get married now. We'll—"

Jerking her hand from his grasp, Joanie bolted to her feet and twisted around to face him. Her lips trembled with barely controlled rage. "Now?" she repeated angrily. "*Now* we can get married?" She clenched her hands tightly at her sides as she struggled to keep from slugging him. "Do you really think that just because you've suddenly realized that you can manage the farm and a family that I'll marry you? Well, you're wrong, J.D. Dead wrong. I was married once to a man who ran every time he was confronted with something that he couldn't handle. I won't make that mistake again.''

''But, Joanie—''

But she wouldn't listen to him anymore. She couldn't. She'd been there Christmas morning, witnessed the disappointment on her children's faces when they'd realized J.D. was gone. They'd wanted to wait for him, but Joanie had insisted they open their presents without him, because she hadn't known when—or even if—he was coming home.

J.D.'s disappearance without a word of explanation had been a cold, bitter reminder of other times she'd been left to cope on her own.

When he reached for her, she backed away, tucking her hands behind her back. ''No!'' she repeated more firmly. ''I want more out of a marriage than a man's sense of duty. I want love, commitment, for both me and my kids.'' When he started to say something, she slung a hand up, stopping him. ''When this baby's born, I'm going home. To *my* home,'' she repeated for what seemed the hundredth time. ''Nothing you can say will change that.''

J.D. shoveled sausages onto a platter, then looked back over his shoulder when the swinging door squeaked open behind him. The twins's faces appeared in the narrow opening. They seemed hesitant to enter, as if unsure of their welcome. J.D. realized then that he'd hurt them as much as their mother with his unexpected departure.

He forced a smile. ''Good morning! You guys hungry?''

They stepped through the door, then stopped, letting

it swing shut behind them. "Yeah," Marissa murmured, licking her lips. "But Mama usually cooks our breakfast. Where is she?"

"Still asleep, I guess." He waved them on in with his spatula. "But don't worry. I'm a pretty good hand in the kitchen, even if I do say so myself." He crossed to the table and pulled out a chair. "Why don't you sit here, sugar?"

Marissa eased his way as if wary. But when she saw the brightly wrapped package in the seat, her eyes bugged wide and she made a wild grab for it. "Is this for me?" she squealed.

J.D. tipped the card up and pretended to study it. "I believe it is." He pulled out another chair and lifted a similarly shaped package. "And I believe this one has Shane's name on it." When Shane hesitated, J.D. nudged him in the chest with the present. "Better open it up, cowboy. You might like what you find inside."

Unable to resist, Shane snatched the package from J.D.'s hands and began to tear off paper. With a head start on her brother, Marissa made short work of the Christmas wrap and lifted the box's lid. Her mouth opened in surprise. "Oh, J.D.!" She lifted out the baby doll cradled in the box. "She's beautiful!" She dropped the doll back in the box and threw her arms around J.D.'s waist.

Laughing, he caught her up under the arms and brought her all the way to his chest. But he wasn't prepared for the emotion that rose in his throat when he felt her tiny arms slip around his neck, when her puckered mouth pressed against his cheek.

He cleared his throat. "I thought since your mama's having a baby, you might like to have one, too."

Shane's fingers froze on his present as he listened to this exchange. J.D. tossed back his head and laughed at the trepidation he saw in the boy's eyes. "Don't worry, Shane. You won't find a baby doll in your box."

The boy sagged with relief. He tore off the lid and dug through tissue paper, sending it flying, until he found the tooled leather belt. "Wow!" he cried, pulling it out. "A belt!" Then he saw the letters carved across the back, and he looked up at J.D., his eyes round, his mouth forming a silent "oh."

Emotion clotted in J.D.'s throat once again. He laid a hand on the boy's shoulder. "You earned it, son."

Shane's cheeks turned beet red as he fought tears and he quickly turned his gaze back to the belt before J.D. saw the sissy display. "Shane," he read aloud, as if unable to believe it. He swiped his sleeve beneath his eyes, then looked back up at J.D. "It's just like yours, 'cept it has my name. Thanks, J.D."

The hinges on the swinging door squeaked again, and all three turned to see Joanie standing in the doorway. J.D.'s heart swelled at the sight of her. He'd made a mistake the night before when he'd asked her to marry him. He wouldn't make it again. He'd give her a little time to cool off, then he'd tell her how much he loved her and her kids.

Marissa wiggled in J.D.'s arms and he lowered her to the floor. Both children dashed to their mother, thrusting their gifts at her. "Look, Mama!" they cried in unison. "See what J.D. gave us!"

Joanie lifted her gaze to J.D.'s over the tops of her children's heads, then dropped to her knees to admire the children's bounty. "Oh, what a beautiful baby!" she murmured. "Have you named her yet?"

"No. Have you picked a name for yours?"

"No, not yet."

"Then we'll name them together," Marissa promised, hugging the doll to her chest.

Joanie turned her attention to her son. "And would you look at that? A real cowboy belt!" She took the belt and threaded it through the loops of her son's jeans, hampered by her trembling fingers. She fastened it snugly in place, then leaned back. "You look like a real cowboy now."

Shane spun, his head dipped over his shoulder as he struggled to see the back.

J.D. clapped his hands together and rubbed enthusiastically. "How about some breakfast? I've got sausages and scrambled eggs ready. Joanie?" He held out a chair for her. She almost sat down before she saw the gift tucked on the seat. She straightened, her eyes darting to J.D.'s. He picked up the package and placed it in her hands. "Merry Christmas, Joanie," he murmured.

She reached for the small, brightly wrapped package and their fingers brushed. She glanced up and their eyes met and she nearly melted at the look of nervous expectation in his eyes. Unable to trust her knees to support her any longer, she sagged onto the chair. J.D. hunkered down at her side, watching. Her fingers trembled on the red ribbon, making unwrapping almost impossible.

Pressed against her mother's shoulder, Marissa prodded, "Hurry, Mama!"

After finally managing to remove the ribbon, she

slipped a nail beneath the seam of the gold foil wrapping and eased off the Scotch tape. She had to take a breath before she could find the courage to lift the lid on the small velvet box. It snapped back on hinges, revealing a ring nestled in white satin. On the band of gold, two emeralds caught the light and sparkled.

"It's a mother's ring," J.D. explained. He took the ring from the box, then took Joanie's right hand in his. Her vision blurred as he slipped it on her finger, his touch burning hot against her chilled flesh. "A birthstone for Marissa and one for Shane. And there's room to add another stone when our baby's born."

Our baby? Joanie tensed. Is that what he'd said? She struggled to concentrate. He'd never referred to the baby as anything but that—the baby. She tried to stifle the bubble of hope that bloomed to life in her heart. Could it be that he had feelings for this child they shared, feelings he was only just beginning to understand? She remembered their conversation of the night before when he'd told her that actually feeling the baby move had given it a sense of reality for him that he hadn't known before. In a way, she could understand that. Almost from conception, a woman was aware of the baby's existence, her body changing and growing right along with the growth of the baby.

She laid a hand on her protruding stomach and squeezed back tears, grateful that at least this child would receive J.D.'s love.

She stared at the ring and the strong male fingers that still held it in place. "Thank you, J.D.," she whispered. "You couldn't have given me anything I would cherish more."

* * *

As soon as breakfast was over, J.D. headed for the barn and his morning chores, wearing a worn denim jacket over the vest Joanie had knitted for him as a gift from her and the children. Their voices raised in excitement, Marissa and Shane skipped along behind him, trying to keep up with his long stride.

Joanie washed the dishes and straightened the kitchen, then went through the house putting things away and making beds. As she tucked the bedspread beneath the pillows on her bed, she felt the scrape of the ring's stones against the cover's quilted squares. Crossing to the window, she held up her hand, studying the jewels in the sunlight. The two emeralds representing the month of May in which the twins were born caught the light and shimmered before her eyes. She curled her fingers against her palm, felt the warmth of the gold band that circled her finger, then brought it to her heart.

As she stared out the window, in the distance she could see Shane staggering drunkenly as he dragged a bale of hay to the truck where J.D. worked throwing the bales onto its bed. Marissa sat on the stacked hay behind the truck's cab, her feet swinging merrily from her high perch. Joanie thought of the gifts J.D. had given her children, the thoughtfulness in each selection.

If only... She caught herself before the thought could fully form. "No," she murmured with a shake of her head as she turned her back to the window. Life wasn't lived on "if onlys."

She headed toward the kitchen and the pile of dirty clothes waiting for her in the laundry room. Halfway down the hall she stumbled, slamming a hand against the wall and curling the other beneath the baby's weight as a pain knifed through her back and shot through her middle. She bent forward on a low groan. *It can't be,* she thought hysterically. *The baby's not due for weeks.* She waited, her breath coming in harsh, dragging gasps, for the pain to ease. After a long, sweat-producing moment, it passed. She slowly straightened, still bracing a hand against the wall. Braxton Hicks, she told herself as she carefully made her way to the kitchen. She remembered well the false labor pains she'd experienced before the twins were born.

She made it as far as the kitchen table before another pain ripped through her. She felt the spurt of warm moisture between her legs and her eyes widened in horror.

J.D.! I've got to get J.D.

J.D. pulled off his gloves and stuck them in his back pocket as he grinned up at Marissa and Shane. The twins sat atop the hay on the back of the truck, their cheeks rosy from the cold. "You guys gonna' ride back here?"

"Can we?" Shane asked hopefully.

J.D. laughed. "I suppose. We're not going far." He patted his jacket pocket for his keys but didn't find the familiar bulge. Then he remembered tossing them onto the kitchen counter the night before. "Sit tight a minute, kids," he told the twins. "I've got to run back to the house and get the keys."

He jogged toward the house, anxious to get the morning's chores behind him so that he could talk to Joanie. And this time he'd make her listen. If he had his way, there would be a wedding before the new year dawned. He pushed open the back door and closed it quickly behind him to keep out the cold air and immediately reached for the keys on the counter. He froze when he caught a glimpse of Joanie stooped beside the kitchen table, her knuckles white as she gripped its polished oak top.

"Joanie?" he murmured as he slowly crossed to her. "Honey, are you all right?"

She lifted her head then, and he saw the perspiration that dampened the hair at her temples. Her lips were pressed tightly together and tears streaked her cheeks. He was at her side in a flash, wrapping an arm around her shaking shoulders.

"Honey, what is it?"

"The baby," she managed to gasp out. "It's coming."

J.D.'s eyes widened. "Now? But it isn't due for weeks."

Fresh tears welled in Joanie's eyes. "Tell *him* that!" she cried.

J.D. eased her toward a chair, stretching behind her to pluck the phone from the wall. "You just sit tight and take it easy. I'll take care of everything." He quickly punched in Manuel's number. "Lupe, it's J.D. Joanie's in labor. Can you get down here fast?" Without waiting for an answer, he slammed the phone back on its cradle.

"The children," Joanie said between moans.

"Don't worry about them," he soothed. "They're sitting on the hay in the truck. Lupe'll take care of them." He glanced around, not sure what to do. "Do you have a bag packed?"

"No," Joanie wailed. "I hadn't thought I'd need one so soon."

J.D. patted her shoulder. "Don't worry. We'll get you some things later. Right now, we need to get you to the hospital. Do you think you can make it all the way to Georgetown?"

She nodded and J.D. prayed she was right. He might have delivered his share of foals, but he didn't know beans about bringing a baby into the world.

Chapter Ten

By the time J.D. and Joanie made it outside, Lupe had arrived and had a twin by each hand. The children broke from her grasp and ran to Joanie as soon as they saw their mother crossing the lawn.

"Mama! Mama!" Marissa called out as she ran. "Where are you going?"

Joanie forced a cheerful smile and stopped to drape an arm around her daughter's shoulder. "To the hospital, sweetheart, to have the baby."

Marissa's eyes rounded as she peered up at Joanie. "But it's not supposed to come until next year!"

Joanie couldn't help but laugh. Marissa made the baby's scheduled birth date sound like months away instead of only weeks. "That's true, but he's decided to come a little early." She gathered both her children in front of her and tipped up their chins. "Now I want you to be good for Lupe and mind what she says.''

"Yes, ma'am," they murmured in unison.

"And no fighting."

"No, ma'am, we'll be good."

Tears burned and she gathered them close for a hug. They wrapped their arms around her and clung. She felt another contraction tighten her swollen stomach and she reached across their heads for J.D.'s hand. His knees nearly buckled at the strength of her grip.

"We'd better go," she told him, not wanting to frighten the children by allowing them to see her in pain. With a quick kiss to the top of each twin's head, she separated herself from them and shooed them toward Lupe, then with J.D.'s help climbed into the truck. As they drove away, she turned to glance over her shoulder for one last glimpse of her children, but the hay stacked high in the bed of the truck blocked her view. Tears flooding her eyes, she turned around and clenched her teeth against the pain.

J.D. glanced at the clock on the dash. "Three minutes apart. Are you sure you can make it?"

Joanie closed her fingers around the seat's edge and gave him a tense nod as she stared through the windshield, focusing on the road ahead to escape the pain. The ride over the country roads was a nightmare for Joanie, each bump drawing a pain-filled groan. Hay bales bounced from the speeding truck and fell to the road behind them to lay like giant bread crumbs scattered to mark the way back home. Once they hit the highway, J.D. pressed the accelerator to the floor. He reached for Joanie's hand and her fingers closed around his like a vice.

He made the forty-five-minute drive to Georgetown in thirty and none too soon. By the time he wheeled in front of the emergency room, the pains were two minutes apart. His heart pounding loudly enough to wake the dead, he jumped from the truck and raced inside, returning seconds later shoving a wheelchair in front of him and dragging a nurse by the hand.

"Okay, honey," he soothed, cupping Joanie's elbow and helping her down. "Everything's going to be all right now." He guided her gently into the wheelchair, then turned, wheeling it at a fast clip for the entrance.

Once inside, he hesitated, not sure which direction to go. The nurse calmly and forcibly shouldered him aside. "We'll take over from here," she assured him.

"Oh-h-h-h-h," Joanie moaned and doubled over. J.D. was at her side in a flash. He pried one of her hands from the arm of the wheelchair and clung as he jogged along beside her.

"Sir!" a voice called from behind him. "Sir! Please wait! You've got to fill out the paperwork to admit her."

J.D. cast a furtive glance over his shoulder to see a woman waving a fistful of papers at him. He started to turn back, but Joanie tightened her fingers around his hand, her grip desperate as she clung to him. J.D. felt like he was being ripped in two. He knew he needed to get Joanie admitted, but he knew, too, that Joanie needed him with her. And that's where he wanted to be. With Joanie.

The wheelchair stopped and so did J.D. He dropped to a knee beside it. He covered their joined hands with his other. "Joanie, I've got to get you admitted. You hang on and I'll be with you as quick as I can."

He could see the fear in her eyes, the pain, and hated like hell leaving her. He kissed her quickly, then rose and stepped back, the onward momentum of the wheelchair wrenching her hand from his.

He turned and ran for the desk and the admitting clerk who waited for him. He dragged a chair to the desk. "Make it fast," he ordered fiercely.

Taken aback, the woman quickly shuffled through papers. "Patient's name?"

"Joanie Summers."

"Middle name?"

He frowned. "I don't know."

The clerk frowned, too. "Birth date?"

J.D.'s frown quickly turned into a scowl as he realized how little he knew about Joanie…other than that he loved her, of course. He knew the twins' birth date, but that had been easy to get out of Marissa when he'd needed to know their birth date for the ring he'd bought Joanie. Marissa loved to talk. "I don't know," he said, his frustration growing. "Is this really important? She's having our baby, for God's sake. I need to be with her."

"The paperwork has to be completed before we can officially admit her. Has she ever been a patient in our hospital before?"

J.D. dragged a shaking hand down his face, remembering her fall from the ladder. "Yes. In September."

The clerk turned to the computer on her desk and began hitting the keys. She stared at the screen as names scrolled by, then glanced questioningly at J.D. "Joan Hill Summers?"

J.D. felt his breath ease out of him in relief. "Yes, ma'am. That's her."

Once Joanie's name had been located in the hospital's computer system, the admission proceeded without a hitch. Within minutes, J.D. was striding down the corridor, studying numbered plates on doors, looking for the room where he'd been told he'd find Joanie.

At last he located it and knocked softly. A strange female voice called, "Come on in."

J.D. pushed open the door a crack and peered inside. Sure enough, there sat Joanie, already draped in a hospital gown, her arm outstretched while the nurse poked a needle into the vein at her wrist. He quickly crossed to the opposite side of the bed, dragging his hat off his head. He tossed it to a chair and gathered Joanie's other hand in his. "You doing okay?" he asked softly.

She nodded, her lips trembling.

"You made it just in time," the nurse told J.D. "We're on our way to the delivery room."

"Delivery room!" he exclaimed, jerking his gaze to the nurse. "Already?"

The nurse finished wrapping a piece of white tape around the needle hanging from Joanie's wrist. "This little lady doesn't waste any time." She tested the bag of fluid hanging from the IV stand beside the bed. Satisfied, she let it drop back into place, then moved to place a hand on Joanie's stomach. "Here comes another one," the nurse warned, then looked up at J.D. "Are you going into the delivery room with her?"

J.D.'s eyes widened and his face paled. He'd never considered the fact that he might actually be asked to witness the birth of his child. He dropped his gaze to Joanie. Her eyes were closed and her lips were pinched into a tight white line as she slowly breathed deeply through her nose. He knew then that he'd go to hell and back for her if she wanted him to. "If Joanie wants me," he replied uncertainly.

"Yes," she gasped, then went back to her breathing.

"Well, then, you'll need to change into a surgical gown. There's one in the bathroom," the nurse said, pointing behind her. "Put on the mask, the hat and then slip the cloth booties over your own boots. But you better be quick about it."

J.D. dashed away, his heart thundering in his chest like a herd of wild horses. When he returned, the nurse had raised the guardrails on the gurney and was waiting by the door. She grinned at J.D. "It's show time."

J.D. followed the gurney through double doors and into a sparsely fitted room that gleamed in stainless steel. While the nurses shifted Joanie from one bed to another, J.D. tried his best to stay out of the way. But once she was settled, he was by her side, grabbing for her hand. He brushed the dampened strands of hair from her face. "You doing okay?" he asked nervously.

She tried to smile her reassurance, then winced, her body tensing as another contraction started.

"Another one?" the nurse asked as she shimmied a sheet up over Joanie's knees.

"Yes!" Joanie gasped, her face contorted in pain.

"Don't fight. Go with it. Pant. It'll help."

Joanie puffed like a two-year-old trying to blow out birthday candles until her face turned beet red.

The double doors swung open and Doc Reynolds pushed his way into the delivery room. "Joanie Summers, I swear, don't you know how to read a calendar?"

Joanie tried to smile again, and J.D. could see how relieved she was to know her physician was there. "I do, but unfortunately, this baby can't read yet."

Doc chortled as he wheeled a stool to the foot of the bed. He glanced J.D.'s way and nodded. "Are you here to help or watch?"

Help? J.D. swallowed hard. "You mean deliver the baby?"

Doc tossed back his head and laughed. "No, I can handle that part. You just do what you can to keep Joanie comfortable."

Short of trading places with her on the bed, which he'd do in a heartbeat if that were possible, J.D. wasn't sure how he could accomplish that. He tightened his hand on Joanie's.

After checking Joanie's progress, the doctor stood and adjusted a mirror suspended from the ceiling. "The baby's head has crowned." He tapped a knuckle against the mirror. "You can watch the action from up here."

Joanie let out a low groan, her grip on J.D.'s tightening until he was sure a bone would snap. "Another contraction?" he asked, knowing how stupid the question must sound.

She caught her lower lip between her teeth and nodded. Tears rolled down her cheeks.

"Joanie, when I give you the word, I want you to

push. Ready?'' Doc Reynolds asked. He waited a couple of beats, then ordered, ''Push!''

She rose off the pillows, growling low in her throat
and J.D. quickly braced her with a hand to her back
as she strained, pushing with all her strength.

''Good girl,'' Doc praised and Joanie collapsed
back against the pillow, her chest heaving. But before
she could get a good breath, he ordered, ''Now push
again.''

Exhausted already, Joanie shook her head. ''I
can't.''

''Come on, honey,'' J.D. urged. ''You can do it.''
He stole a glance in the mirror and saw the baby's
head. ''Oh, Joanie, honey, look!'' he cried, awed by
the sight. ''He's almost here.''

Joanie looked into the mirror, and with J.D.'s help
she pushed herself from the pillow, straining for all
she was worth, perspiration beading her forehead. J.D.
mopped at it frantically with a wet cloth a nurse
pressed into his hand. He stole another glance at the
mirror and saw the baby's shoulders appear.

''Another good push and we'll have him,'' Doc
said.

J.D. held Joanie upright, his cheeks pressed against
hers, straining right along with her. The miracle that
unfolded before his eyes stole his breath. Shoulders,
arms, torso, a little behind. By the time two feet appeared kicking wildly, he was almost laughing. ''My
God! Joanie, would you look at that?''

Joanie was laughing, too, while tears streamed down
her face. Doc quickly clamped the umbilical cord, then
rounded the bed to place the baby on Joanie's stomach.

"You've got yourself another healthy boy," Doc said proudly. Awed, J.D. could do nothing but stare while Joanie reached out and touched the tiny fingers that fanned the air.

"Oh, J.D., isn't he beautiful?" she murmured.

"Yeah…" J.D. had to swallow back the emotion that clogged his throat. He tightened his arm around Joanie, pressing first his lips then his cheek against hers. "A son," he said softly, testing the sound of the words. He stretched out an unsteady hand to cradle the baby's wet head. "Would you get a load of that hair?" he said. "I swear, he's got more than me."

Joanie laughed, though she sounded tired. "He'll probably lose most of it."

J.D. jerked his hand back. "Lose it!" he croaked.

Joanie chuckled at the look of surprise on his face. "Don't worry. It'll grow back."

Relieved, J.D. poked a finger at his son's hand and was rewarded when the baby curled four tiny fingers around his. "Would you look at that?" he said, grinning like a fool. "He's strong as an ox."

A nurse appeared by the side of the bed. "I hate to interrupt this little party, but we need to get him weighed and measured and give him a bath." J.D. watched the nurse wrap a blanket around the baby, then followed her until she reached a door. "You can't go in here," she scolded gently. J.D. held the door as the nurse and his son passed through, feeling oddly abandoned.

He turned back to Joanie and found another nurse had taken his place at her side. "We've some work to do yet," she told J.D. "If you'd like, you can wait for her in her room. We shouldn't be too long."

He shifted his gaze to Joanie and she smiled reassuringly at him. "Don't worry. I'll be fine."

J.D. paced Joanie's small hospital room, watching the minute hand on the wall clock crawl past the numbers. When thirty minutes had passed with no sign of Joanie, he was about ready to head back to the delivery room to see what was taking so long. But then the door opened and a nurse came in, pushing a portable bassinet in front of her.

"Oh!" she said, looking at J.D. in surprise. "Your wife's not back yet?"

J.D. didn't even bother to correct the woman by telling her that Joanie wasn't his wife because he intended to rectify that little problem as soon as Joanie was feeling up to it. "No, ma'am." He tiptoed to the side of the crib and peered down at his son. A broad smile spread across his face at the angelic sight before him. Cleaned and dressed, the baby was wrapped up tighter than a papoose in a light blue blanket. "Is he sleeping?" he whispered.

"Probably, but not for long. You can hold him if you like."

Before J.D. could tell her thanks but no thanks, she'd scooped the baby from the bassinet and plopped him into J.D.'s arms. His eyes widened. "He hardly weighs a thing!" he exclaimed in a loud whisper. "It's like holding air."

The nurse simply laughed. "Your wife would probably disagree with that. He weighed in at almost nine pounds. No telling how much he would have weighed if she'd carried him full term."

J.D. couldn't take his eyes off the cherubic face

tipped up to his. "He's okay, isn't he? I mean, coming early didn't hurt him, did it?"

"No," she assured him. "He's fit as a fiddle." She pushed the bassinet out of the way, then headed for the door. "Y'all just visit awhile, get to know each other. Your wife should be back any minute. If you need anything, just press the buzzer." With that advice she was gone.

And J.D. was alone with his son for the first time.

He puckered his lips and blew out a long, nervous breath. "Well, big guy, it's just you and me now," he said, unsure what to do with the bundle he held in his arms. He crossed to the window, keeping his steps careful and slow as if he were carrying a basket of eggs instead of a baby. "Want to get a look at the world you've been born into?" he asked. He cradled his son higher on his arm so he could see the view out the window. He chuckled when his son's eyes remained closed. "I guess you're pretty worn out after the trip you just made," he said in understanding. He sighed and shifted the baby to his chest. "To be honest, I'm pretty exhausted myself. But your mother now," he added judiciously, "she's the one who should be tired. After all, she did all the work."

He studied his son's face in the late-afternoon sunlight, noting the rosy color of his cheeks and the mass of hair that had been combed and slicked into place. He looked for a resemblance to himself. The nose, he decided, and the shape of his chin. Those were definitely Cawthon features. If possible, his chest swelled a little bigger.

"You are one lucky hombre," he told the baby. "Your mama is the absolute best. You're gonna love her," he said, unashamed of the tears that misted his eyes. "But in case you have any doubts, you can get verification from Marissa and Shane. That's your sister and your brother," he explained. At that moment, the door opened and J.D. turned to see the foot of the hospital bed appear in the doorway. "Well, here she is son," he murmured as he watched the nurse wheel the bed into the room.

Joanie lifted her head at the sound of J.D.'s voice, then pushed to her elbows when she saw who he held. "Oh, let me see him," she cried.

J.D. stepped out of the way while the nurse slid Joanie's bed in place, then moved to her side, unable to stop a wide grin from crossing his face. "He's a keeper," he said, unable to mask his pride.

Joanie held out her hands and J.D. carefully transferred the baby to her arms. "Hello, precious," she cooed, rearranging the blanket around the baby's face for a better view. She lifted her face to J.D., her face wreathed in the most beautiful smile J.D. had ever seen. "We did good, didn't we?" she asked.

"Damn good," he agreed, angling a hip on the side of the bed beside them and bracing an arm along the bed's back, unable to allow any more distance than that between them.

The nurse chuckled softly as she listened to the exchange. She completed her adjustments to the drip bag, then headed for the door. "I'll get out of y'all's hair. But if you need anything—"

"Press the buzzer," Joanie and J.D. voiced in unison, then they looked at each other and laughed. The nurse just chuckled again and shook her head as she pulled open the door.

Once they were alone, J.D. turned to Joanie, the smile melting away. His face held a seriousness, an intensity about it that Joanie hadn't seen before.

"Thank you," he murmured, slipping his arm around her shoulders and gathering her close. "I..." When words failed him, he repeated, "Thank you," and buried his lips in the still-damp hair above her ear. He drew away and shifted on the bed until he faced her. He brought his hands to her cheeks, cupping them along her jaw and shaping her face toward his. Joanie felt his hands tremble as his blue eyes bored into hers. "I love you, Joanie," he whispered. "I love you so much."

Joanie felt as if her heart would fly right out of her chest. Never once in the months they'd been together had she heard him voice those words aloud. And, oh, how she'd wanted, needed to hear them. She closed her fingers around his hand and drew it to her lips. "I love you, too, J.D.," she murmured in return.

Though J.D. had wanted to stay the night with her at the hospital, Joanie insisted that he go home and tell the twins about their new brother and get a good night's rest, assuring him that she planned to do the same in preparation for her discharge from the hospital the next day. And she did sleep...at least for a couple of hours.

But some time after midnight, she awakened, her nightgown soaked with perspiration and a knot of fear twisting in her stomach. Her heart pounding like a frantic jackhammer against her ribs, she struggled to pull herself to a sitting position. She switched on the night-light on the panel above the bed, trying to figure out what had awakened her. Had the baby cried out? she wondered, looking toward the bassinet. Whipping back the covers, she let down the side rail on her bed, then slipped to the floor and padded on bare feet to the bassinet parked against the wall. Her son lay sleeping peacefully on his stomach, his left cheek turned toward her.

She tucked the blanket more firmly around him and started to return to her bed, sure that what had awakened her had not been him. Then she thought to herself, phooey, he'd be awake in a little while anyway, so she scooped him up and carried him back to bed with her.

She climbed under the covers, then settled herself against propped pillows while cradling the baby in the crook of her arm. Bringing a fist to his mouth, he nestled contentedly against her breast and suckled. She watched him sleep, and gradually the tightness in her stomach eased and the fear slowly evaporated into a forgotten mist. Unable to resist, she folded back the blanket and counted ten toes, ten fingers, then placed the tentative pad of one finger on the baby's cheek. His head immediately turned, his mouth opening like a hungry bird, waiting for a worm. A smile tipped up the corners of her mouth.

"You look just like your daddy," she whispered to him, admiring the same features J.D. had already pointed out to her and claimed as Cawthon traits. Memories of the time they'd shared together while they had laughed and cooed over their son washed over her. She couldn't remember ever seeing J.D. so free with his emotions, so utterly content as when he'd held his son in his arms.

He'd told her he'd loved her, she remembered and let the treasured words play through her mind and her heart. She'd wanted so much to hear him say those words that she had accepted them as the gift they were without any thought to what had spawned that declaration. But now in the semidarkness of her hospital room, alone except for the babe in her arms, the knot of fear returned to twist like a fist in her stomach. She realized then what had awakened her—not the baby stirring in his bassinet, but the memory of those words.

She'd been so overwhelmed by the excitement and joy of the birth of their son and sharing it all with J.D. that she hadn't really thought about his timing when he'd said the words she'd longed to hear.

But now she did…and she understood.

Like her, J.D. had been running on adrenaline, caught up in the drama of watching his first son being born. The declaration of love, she was sure, had been spontaneous, spoken without thought. The realization saddened her, and she struggled to steel herself against the painful disappointment that squeezed her heart.

She didn't blame J.D. How could she, when that same adrenaline had pumped through her veins, blinding her to everything but those precious moments when they'd shared the thrill of the birth of their son? His excitement had been contagious, his pride in his son obvious, and she'd responded to that, even drawn on it, needing his strength and the warmth of his attention.

It was understandable, even forgivable, that he'd tell her that he loved her. At the time, she was sure he might even have meant it. After all, she'd just given him a son and what man wouldn't feel gratitude for such a gift?

But Joanie was nothing if not a realist. She knew that guilt had fostered his first proposal of marriage and it was a sense of obligation that had forced him to take her and her children into his home. His words of love were nothing but meaningless patter, spoken impulsively and without thought. He probably already regretted saying them. She wouldn't let herself believe anything else. She couldn't. She didn't think she could survive the heartbreak, the disappointment, if she did.

The baby stirred, and she glanced down to see his tiny fist beating the air and the beginnings of a loud, hungry cry building on his red face. Quickly, she eased open her gown and bared a swollen breast. Cooing softly to her son, she positioned him, guiding him to her nipple. Instinctively, he latched on and immediately began to suckle, nudging at her breast with a tight fist.

"But I have you," she whispered, bending to press a kiss on her son's forehead while tears stung her eyes. "The best of both of us. And that will have to be enough."

Joanie heard the door open behind her, but purposely kept her back turned toward it as she forced her stiff fingers to tug the clean diaper into place. She wouldn't let her emotions take over. Not this time. She needed to remain in control. She heard a thump, a light rustling, then the scrape of boots on the polished floor. She sensed J.D. standing behind her, more than felt him, until his nose bumped her chin. She sucked in a steadying breath just before she felt his lips, still carrying the chill of outdoors, brush the column of her neck.

"Good morning," he murmured, his voice vibrating husky and warm against her skin. His arm slipped around her waist. "How are mother and baby doing this morning?"

Joanie fought the urge to turn in his arms. Instead, she pressed the tape into place against the disposable diaper, keeping her gaze on her work. "Fine." She turned then, not into his arms as her heart demanded, but away. "Did you bring the things I asked for?" she asked, stepping back.

J.D. frowned and watched her move away, puzzled by her coolness. "Yeah," he murmured. "The stuff's on the bedside table." He watched while she pulled the items from the bag he'd brought and spread them on the bed, wondering what had happened to the happy, loving woman he'd left the night before. "Joanie?" he asked, crossing to stand behind her. He placed a hand on her shoulder. "Is something wrong?"

He felt her tense, but she didn't move away.

"No," she said with a quick shake of her head. "Nothing. I just need to get the baby dressed is all."

He caught her hand before she could slip by him again. "Can it wait just a minute? I—I have something for you." When she continued to hesitate, he cupped his hand on her shoulder, turning her around to face him, and at the same time pulled his other hand from behind his back.

Joanie's eyes filled with tears at the sight of the roses that seemed to bloom from his hand. She'd never received flowers from a man, not even during her six years of marriage. That she would receive them now, when she was determined to keep her heart and emotions under control, seemed somehow unfair. "Oh, J.D.," she murmured, her voice shaking, "you didn't need to bring me flowers."

"No, but I wanted to." He pressed them toward her. "They reminded me of you," he said gently. "All soft and feminine. I figured roses were your favorite since you wear rose-scented perfume. But if you'd prefer something else—"

"No. No." Joanie took the bouquet from him and buried her face in the velvet petals, inhaling the sensuous fragrance of the fresh-cut blooms. She lifted her head and finally looked at J.D. for the first time since he'd entered the room. She saw the confusion in his eyes, the uncertainty, and wondered if she'd been wrong. No, she quickly told herself. The flowers, like the proposals he'd offered, were given out of a sense of duty. "Thank you, J.D. They're beautiful." She turned away, laying the roses on the bedside table, then picked up a piece of paper. "The nurse came by a few minutes ago and left this form for us to fill out. We need to choose a name for him."

"A name?" he repeated, casting a furtive glance in the direction of the bassinet. He hadn't given any thought to a name.

"Yes. Do you have a preference?"

He turned back to her, and his eyes, blue as the Texas sky, burned clear to her soul. "Only for the last one."

She swallowed hard, already fearing what he would say. "Oh?"

"Yeah. I'd like for him to have the name Cawthon.

In fact—'' he stepped closer, and she automatically took a step back, her legs hitting the side of the bed, ''I want to share my name with all of you. I want to marry you, Joanie. I want you to be my wife in every sense of the word. And if their dad's willing, I'd like to share my name with Marissa and Shane, too. I talked to them about it last night and—''

Joanie felt the blood drain from her face at the mention of her children. ''You did what!''

''I talked to them. You know, about us getting married and all, and I mentioned that if they wanted to and their dad agreed, I could adopt them so we'd all have the same last name.''

Joanie's breath came out on a hiss through clenched teeth. ''You talked to my children about us getting married?''

''Well, yeah.'' He grinned nervously. ''Since your dad's not here for me to ask for your hand, I figured they were the next best thing.''

''How dare you!'' she cried, slapping the paper back on the table. ''To discuss this with *my* children before discussing it with me first. I won't have them hurt.''

''Hurt?'' he echoed in disbelief. ''I wouldn't harm a hair on either of those kids' heads!''

''Not intentionally, maybe, but you don't know how difficult it was for them when their father left.''

''Hellfire!'' he exclaimed. ''I'm talking marriage and adoption and you're talking leaving. Are you hearing anything that I've said? I want to marry you. I love you.''

I love you. Those words again. She whirled away in

frustration, digging her fingers through her hair. She couldn't let them affect her judgment.

He took a step toward her, just close enough to touch her lightly on the arm, and when she would have jerked away, he tightened his grip. This time, he'd make her listen. "I didn't do a very good job of proposing before. I haven't had much practice in that department. But I do love you, Joanie. I want you to be my wife."

She snatched her arm from his grasp and pressed her fingers over her ears as if she could block out the words. "You think you love me," she said, her voice thick with accusation. "But you don't."

He blinked and looked at her in surprise. "I don't?"

"No!" she cried, turning to face him. "Don't you see? We experienced a miracle together. The birth of our son. Your emotions are running at an all-time high. You say that you love me, and that you want to marry me, and I believe you really think you do. But once the excitement and novelty die down and reality sets in, you'll regret those words. Believe me, J.D., I know."

"I'm not going to change my mind," he argued. "I do love you and I do want to marry you."

She closed her eyes for a moment, fighting for patience, for a calm she didn't think she'd ever know again. "You proposed to me the first time six months ago and that proposal was delivered out of nothing but pure guilt. You felt responsible, obligated because of the baby. And when I turned your offer down, you felt nothing but relief."

Though he would have liked to have told her she was wrong, J.D. knew it would be a lie. He hadn't loved her then, at least not like he did now. His love for her had grown slowly, unfolding over time like the petals of a rose. "That's true," he admitted reluctantly. "Or at least it was then. But that's not what I feel now."

Joanie stifled a groan and snatched up an infant's gown from the things spread on the bed.

J.D. watched her stomp over to the bassinet, toss the gown over the top rung, then bend and start stuffing diapers from the tray beneath it into her bag. Anger built inside him until he thought he'd burst. He closed the distance between them in two long strides. He caught her by the elbow and spun her around, sending diapers flying across the room.

"You think you have all the answers, don't you?" he muttered through clenched teeth. "Well, you don't. And I'm a little sick and tired of your analyzing everything I say or do and telling me how I feel. I love you, Joanie, and the baby's arrival has nothing to do with those feelings. I loved you long before the baby was born. I just didn't have the guts to tell you before now. And I love your kids, too, and it pains me for you to think that I'd ever do anything to hurt them."

He took a deep breath and released his hold on her. He stepped back, giving her all the room she wanted, needed. "But I won't ask you again to marry me. The offer's still there, mind you. But it's up to you now to decide whether or not to accept it."

Chapter Eleven

The forty-five-minute drive from the hospital in Georgetown to J.D.'s farm was made in tense silence with J.D. scowling at the windshield and Joanie huddled against the passenger door, her arms crossed protectively beneath her breasts. Strapped into a car seat, their baby son slept peacefully between them, oblivious to his parents' tense mood.

Once they reached the farm, J.D. helped Joanie and the baby inside, then went out to the barns, saying he had work to do and telling her that the kids were over at Lupe's. Alone in the house, Joanie quickly settled the baby in the crib J.D. had set up earlier, then lay down on her own bed, exhausted from the lack of sleep the night before and the added strain of her latest confrontation with J.D.

But sleep evaded her. Her thoughts were troubled,

her heart heavy, while J.D.'s challenge echoed over and over in her mind.

I won't ask you again to marry me. The offer's still there, mind you. But it's up to you now to decide whether or not to accept it.

Accept it! she cried inwardly. But how could she accept his offer of marriage when there was so much at stake? If it were just her, she would have said yes without a second thought. But she had her children to think of...Marissa, Shane and the baby who still lacked a name. They deserved permanence and she wasn't sure how long J.D.'s feelings would last.

"Mama!" She heard Marissa's voice then the slam of the back door and pushed herself to a sitting position.

"Back here," she called. The twins burst through her door, peeling off their coats as they ran. They jumped up on the bed and threw themselves into her open arms. She squeezed them hard. "Oh, but I've missed you two," she said, blinking back tears.

"We missed you, too, Mama" they returned in unison.

Marissa was the first to pull away. "Where's the baby?"

"Asleep in the crib. Want a peek at him?"

Marissa was off the bed and shooting toward the crib. Shane followed at a slower pace. Both stood on tiptoes, their chins propped on the top rail between their hands, to peer over the side.

"He's so little," Marissa whispered loudly.

"Eight pounds and twelve ounces," Joanie told them as she went to stand behind them. She placed a hand on each twin's shoulder. "What do you think of your little brother, Shane?

He shrugged. "He's all right, I guess." He tipped up his face to look at her. "When's he gonna wake up?"

Joanie chuckled. "Soon enough."

Marissa whirled around, her eyes bright with excitement. "Can I hold him?"

"Sure." Joanie waved her daughter toward the bed. "Go sit down and I'll bring him to you." Cooing softly, she gently lifted the baby from the crib and carried him over to Marissa. Supporting his head, she shifted the baby to Marissa's arms, then sat down beside her daughter.

Marissa giggled. "Look. He's sucking on his hand."

"That means he's hungry. He'll be wanting to be fed again before long."

"Can I feed him?" she asked hopefully.

Joanie laughed. "Sorry. But he gets his milk from me."

Marissa's smile crumpled. "Oh."

"You can hold him, though, until it's time." That seemed to satisfy Marissa, but Joanie noticed that Shane hung back, as if unsure of this new little presence in their lives. Joanie patted the mattress beside her. "Come on up here, Shane, and join us."

He climbed up and settled his head against his mother's shoulder.

"What did you name him?" Marissa asked.

"We haven't yet," Joanie murmured, remembering that that was what had led to the angry confrontation with J.D.

Marissa rolled her eyes dramatically. "He's got to have a name," she declared.

"Do you have any suggestions?"

Marissa thought a minute. "There's a boy in my class named Chedrick. That's a pretty neat name."

Shane groaned. "That's a nerdy name."

"Is not!"

"Is too!"

"Okay, okay," Joanie chided gently. "That's enough." She turned to Shane, placing an arm around his shoulder. "What would you suggest?"

He got a devilish gleam in his eye. "Let's name him John Delbert after J.D."

Marissa hooted and Joanie just shook her head. "But that's not J.D.'s name."

"Well, name him J.D., then," he insisted. "We can call him Junior so we don't get 'em mixed up."

There won't be any chance of getting them mixed up, Joanie thought sadly, since the senior J.D. wouldn't be around. A sigh moved her shoulders. "How about if we name him John Derrick, then he'd have J.D.'s initials?"

Marissa's eyes lit up. "Oooo, I like that!" she said. She looked down at her little brother. "John Derrick Cawthon," she repeated, trying the name out.

"Only if J.D. approves," Joanie warned.

Marissa looked back up at Joanie. "I bet he will. He even told us he'd 'dopt us when y'all get married so we could all have his last name. Do you think Daddy will let J.D. 'dopt us and change our name to Cawthon, too?" she asked hopefully.

Joanie felt as if Marissa had reached inside her chest and ripped out her heart. Damn you, J.D., she cried silently, for mentioning this to the twins without asking me first. How could she explain to them that she couldn't marry J.D.? That he wouldn't be adopting them? But before she could think of a response, the baby cried, saving her from having to answer her daughter's difficult question.

"Dinnertime," Joanie said and took the baby from Marissa. She shifted the baby to one arm, unbuttoned her blouse and bared a breast. The newly named John Derrick, immediately latched onto a nipple.

"What's he doing?" Marissa asked curiously, her nose pressed to within an inch of the baby's mouth.

"Drinking his milk. Remember when Esmerelda was a kitten and she nursed from her mommy before we brought her home with us?"

"Yeah."

"Well, that's what the baby's doing." Marissa sighed and settled against her mother's arm to watch. Joanie laughed when she saw Shane curl his nose. She ruffled his hair. "You used to do the same thing," she teased him.

He ducked from beneath her hand. "Gross," he said, putting distance between himself and the baby.

J.D. finished up at the barn and headed back to the house to change clothes. He heard their voices as soon as he stepped through the kitchen door—laughing, giggling, loud whispers—and wished he could be a part of that family bonding. But he wouldn't intrude, he told himself, or rather he couldn't. Not with Joanie determined to keep him on the outside.

His eyes locked straight ahead, he headed down the hall, not trusting himself to so much as glance through the open door, hoping to make it to his bedroom without the twins' spotting him. Unfortunately, Marissa did.

Her voice sang out to him just as he passed Joanie's bedroom door. "Hey, J.D.! Come here! We've named the baby!"

He stopped, hauled in a frustrated breath and turned back. He stepped into the doorway, then stopped, his gaze going immediately to Joanie. She sat on the bed, holding the baby to her breast. At his appearance, she modestly pulled her blouse to cover the baby's head and her bared breast. That small act of modesty angered J.D. in a way he couldn't explain. "Yeah?" he asked, forcing a smile. "What did y'all come up with?"

Marissa choked back a laugh. "Well, Shane wanted to name him John Delbert after you, but Mama thought John Derrick sounded better. That way, the baby would have your initials."

J.D. shot his gaze to Joanie, shocked that after all she'd said she would honor him in that way. "John Derrick," he repeated, the words coming out like a harsh croak. He cleared his throat and tried again. "John Derrick. That has a right nice ring to it."

"Then we can name him that?" Marissa asked in excitement.

"Fine by me," J.D. replied.

"When are we going to change our names?" Marissa asked, shifting her gaze between her mother and J.D.

J.D. sensed Joanie's anger, but he refused to take the heat on this question. If left up to him, the adoption would take place right along with the wedding. He loved the kids as much as he did their mother. He turned his gaze fully on Joanie. "That's up to your mother," he said.

Marissa tipped up her chin to look at her mother. "Mama?" she prodded. "When can we?"

Joanie frowned at J.D., telling him with her eyes how much she resented him dumping this on her. "I don't know, sweetheart," she hedged. "There's a lot to be considered before we take that step."

"Like what?" Marissa persisted, not willing to accept Joanie's feeble excuse.

"Well, your daddy for one thing. I'm not sure how he'd feel about you guys changing your name."

"He wouldn't care," Shane muttered. "He doesn't like us anyway."

Joanie's mouth dropped open. "Shane Summers," she exclaimed, "that simply isn't true!"

Shane scooted off the bed. "Yeah, it is. When we were at Mimi's, I heard him tell Pawpaw we weren't nothin' but a royal pain in the butt."

Joanie's eyes grew round. "Shane Summers! Don't you talk like that!" The baby cried out at Joanie's outburst, releasing his hold on her nipple, and she quickly shifted him to her shoulder and soothed.

Scowling, Shane aligned himself beside J.D. and stuffed his hands in his pockets. He lifted a shoulder in a shrug, staring at his boots. "I was just telling you what he said."

Her emotions and her heart running out of control, Joanie swallowed hard while she patted frantically on the baby's back, trying to calm his cries. "Marissa. Shane. Why don't the two of you go in and watch television for a while and let J.D. and me talk privately for a minute."

"Can we take John Derrick with us?" Marissa asked hopefully.

Though she wondered how she did it, Joanie forced a sympathetic smile. "No, sweetheart. He'd better stay with me right now."

Her face puckered in a pout, Marissa pushed herself off the bed and trailed Shane to the den. As soon as the two were out of earshot, Joanie turned her anger loose on J.D.

"Do you see what you've done?" she all but shouted, trying to keep her voice from carrying. "It's exactly what I've tried so hard to prevent." John Derrick raised his own cries to be heard over Joanie's. "Shhh," she soothed, trying to calm him. J.D. strolled over and took the baby from Joanie's arms. He lifted him to his shoulder and the baby instantly hushed.

That defection of her youngest child to J.D.'s touch angered Joanie all the more. She grabbed the plackets of her blouse and furiously pushed buttons through holes.

"And just exactly what have you tried to prevent?" J.D. asked calmly.

Joanie stood, her cheeks flushed with anger. "I didn't want them to start thinking of you as a replacement for their daddy."

"Neither did I," he replied. "I don't want them thinking I'm anything like their daddy," he added dryly. "In my book, the man's not much of a father."

"Oh? And you'll be a better one?" she asked sarcastically.

"Damn straight." He carried the baby to the crib

and gently laid him down. After tucking the blanket around his son, he turned, his gaze boring into Joanie's. "I love those kids, Joanie. And this one, too," he said with a jerk of his head toward the crib. "And I think they love me, as well. All it takes is the word from you and we can all start being a family in the truest sense of the word."

A family. Joanie rolled to her stomach, a position she hadn't been able to achieve in months, and pressed her fist to her mouth to keep back the sobs that threatened to overcome her. No one wanted a family more than she did. Hadn't she struggled alone for years to provide just that for her children? Even when their father had been around, the burden had been hers to carry. After he'd left, she'd continued to provide for their needs both physically and emotionally. But she had always known a piece of the puzzle had been missing and no matter how hard she tried to fill this, she couldn't. They needed both a father and a mother.

And now J.D. wanted to fill that gap. Did he truly mean the things he'd said? she wondered, her mind swimming in confusion. Were his offers of marriage and adoption spoken out of more than just guilt? She squeezed her eyes shut, unable to allow herself to fully believe.

But the memories were there, whirling in her mind and pushing against her heart. J.D.'s trips to Liberty Hill to check on them, always bringing with him something to lighten her load, whether it was a sack of produce from Lupe's garden, steaks to grill outside, or a crisp one-hundred-dollar-bill left for her to find. Changing her oil, mowing her lawn. Taking Shane and

Marissa for pizza so she could rest. Spending the night on her sofa, watching over them all. Staying with her in the hospital when she'd fallen from the ladder. The Halloween hayride, the Thanksgiving meal and Marissa's words of thanks and the look on J.D.'s face when he had heard them. And Christmas. The gifts he'd chosen so carefully for her children and the ring he'd given her. He couldn't have chosen anything that would have pleased her more.

The memories continued to whirl through her mind until at last exhaustion overtook her and she slept.

J.D., his ear cocked for any sound from Joanie's room, heard the baby when he first began to stir. He rolled from his bed, still dressed in his jeans, and trotted down the short hall that separated his room and Joanie's. Whispering to the baby, he scooped him up, grabbed some diapers and a clean nightgown and headed for the kitchen, determined to let Joanie get the rest she so badly needed.

In the kitchen, he dug through the box of supplies the hospital staff had sent home with them until he found a premixed bottle of formula.

He jiggled the fussing baby in one arm while he grabbed a pan and filled it with water. "Hang on, little guy," he whispered. "We'll get this warm in a minute. In the meantime, let's see if we can get you changed into some dry clothes."

Joanie awakened slowly, dragged from her exhausted slumber by the sound of the baby's cries. Half-asleep, she stumbled to the crib and reached for John Derrick. Her hands found nothing but a tangled blanket. Instantly awake, she lifted her head, listening, and realized the cries had come from somewhere else in the house.

She grabbed her robe from the foot of the bed and slipped it on as she followed the sound to the kitchen. In the doorway, she stopped, her heart climbing slowly to her throat. The only light came from the single fixture that glowed from over the sink. A blanket was spread on the table and next to it lay a wadded and decidedly wet diaper. Strips of white tape were scattered like snow across the dark oak tabletop. Disposable diapers, their plastic outer covering ripped and exposing the cotton batting inside, littered the floor, forgotten.

Beyond the blanket sat the box from the hospital, its cardboard lids folded back. Her gaze drifted to the stove, where J.D. stood with his back to her, wearing nothing but jeans. He held the baby draped over one shoulder, while he shook a baby bottle over his wrist, testing the temperature of the milk. The baby's tiny fists beat his father's wide shoulders while he kept up a heart-rending howl.

At the sight of the two of them, tears burned the back of Joanie's eyes and clotted in her throat. The twins' father had never so much as changed a diaper, much less offered to take on the two o'clock feeding, thereby giving her a few hours extra sleep. Seeing J.D. there, struggling with the crying baby, knowing full well he was doing it for her, accomplished what no words of assurance ever could. He loved them, all of them, just as he'd said.

"J.D.?" she called softly.

He whirled at the sound of her voice, his face

flushed from the heat of the stove and his efforts to quiet the baby. His eyes taking on a guarded look, he frowned when he saw her standing in the kitchen doorway. "Sorry," he mumbled. "I was trying to save you from having to get up." Joanie walked into the kitchen and stooped to pick up the torn diapers from the floor. J.D.'s frown deepened as he watched her. "Ruined a few before I could figure out how the dang contraptions worked," he said in frustration.

Joanie smiled through her tears as she laid the torn diapers on the table. "I can see that." The baby's howls of hunger increased and J.D. ducked a flying fist. Joanie turned, her heart nearly breaking at the sight of the man she loved and the son they'd created together. "Would you like for me to feed him?"

J.D. let out a frustrated breath. "Yeah, I guess you better before he wakes up the whole house."

Joanie stretched out her hands and J.D. passed the baby to her. She sat down in one of the chairs, cooing softly as she adjusted her robe and nightgown. J.D. propped a hip against the kitchen counter and watched.

A nipple appeared, a bead of translucent milk glistening at its tip. Before the breast was fully exposed, the baby latched onto the budded nipple and the crying stopped as he began to greedily suckle. This time, Joanie didn't bother to try to hide her nakedness.

J.D. found himself drawing up a chair beside them. He touched a finger to the baby's cheek and smiled as he felt the baby's jaw move against it. "He's a greedy little devil, isn't he?"

"No more than any other."

J.D. glanced up and found Joanie's gaze on him. His heart tripped then sputtered into a pounding beat

against his ribs at what he thought he saw in her eyes.
Slowly, he drew his hand back, starting to place it on
his thigh, but instead he lifted it to Joanie's face, curving it along her jaw. She closed her eyes and nuzzled
his hand between her shoulder and cheek. A lone tear
leaked out and dripped onto his fingers.

"J.D.—"

"Joanie—"

They both laughed self-consciously as their words
tangled. J.D. hitched a hand beneath the seat of his
chair and drew it closer. "We can make this work,
Joanie," he said earnestly. "If you'll only give me a
chance to prove that I mean what I've said."

Emotion closed Joanie's throat and it was several
moments before she could push out the words she
needed to say beyond the choking tears. "I know, J.D.
Or at least I do now. It took me awhile to believe that
what you said, that what you've done for us, truly
came from your heart. Can you forgive me for being
so stubborn, so blind?"

A soft, loving smile tipped the corners of J.D.'s
mouth. "I might with a little persuasion."

Joanie caught her lower lip between her teeth and
looked down at the child they had created together,
this gift that had brought them together. She lifted her
gaze to his. "I love you, J.D.," she whispered. "I have
for as long as I can remember."

Before the words had fully passed her lips, J.D. was
hauling her, baby and all, onto his lap and into his
arms. The baby fussed at the interruption, then settled
back against Joanie's breast, taking the nipple back
into his mouth once again. J.D. pressed his nose to
Joanie's neck, inhaling the scent of roses that was so

much a part of her. "God, I love you. More than yesterday, but not nearly as much as tomorrow."

Joanie's breath came out of her on a long, heartfelt sigh and she tipped her head to rest on his, accepting his love and allowing it to settle around her. "I want us to be a family, J.D.," she murmured, "just like you said. I want to be your wife and I want you to adopt Marissa and Shane, if their daddy is willing."

He tightened his arms around her, lifting his head to find her lips. The kiss was achingly sweet and full of promises for the future. "Family," he repeated on a sigh when at last he drew away. His gaze touched hers, his blue eyes full of warmth and love and just a little teasing. "I never thought I'd be saying this, but nothing in the world would make me happier."

J.D. pressed his lips against her temple. "Will it always be like this?" he whispered.

Smiling softly, Joanie lifted her gaze to his, her eyes filled with her love for him. "Always."

* * * * *

TRACI ON THE SPOT   BY TRACI

1

Morgan Brigham slowly set down his coffee cup on the kitchen table and stared at the comic strip in the center of his paper. It was nestled in among approximately twenty others that were spread out across two pages. But this was the only one he made a point of reading faithfully each morning at breakfast.

This was the only one that mirrored *her* life.

He read each panel twice, as if he couldn't trust his own eyes. But he could. It was there, in black and white.

Morgan folded the paper slowly, thoughtfully, his mind not on his task. So Traci was getting engaged.

The realization gnawed at the lining of his stomach. He hadn't a clue as to why.

He had even less of a clue why he did what he did next.

Abandoning his coffee, now cool, and the newspaper, and ignoring the fact that this was going to make him late for the office, Morgan went to get a sheet of stationery from the den.

He didn't have much time.

Traci Richardson stared at the last frame she had just drawn. Debating, she glanced at the creature sprawled out on the kitchen floor.

"What do you think, Jeremiah? Too blunt?"

The dog, part bloodhound, part mutt, idly looked up from his rawhide bone at the sound of his name. Jeremiah gave her a look she felt free to interpret as ambivalent.

"Fine help you are. What if Daniel actually reads this and puts two and two together?"

Not that there was all that much chance that the man who had proposed to her, the very prosperous and busy Dr. Daniel Thane, would actually see the comic strip she drew for a living. Not unless the strip was taped to a bicuspid he was examining. Lately Daniel had gotten so busy he'd stopped reading anything but the morning headlines of the *Times*.

Still, you never knew. "I don't want to hurt his feelings," Traci continued, using Jeremiah as a sounding board. "It's just that Traci is overwhelmed by Donald's proposal and, see, she thinks the ring is going to swallow her up." To prove her point, Traci held up the drawing for the dog to view.

This time, he didn't even bother to lift his head.

Traci stared moodily at the small velvet box on the kitchen counter. It had sat there since Daniel had asked her to marry him last Sunday. Even if Daniel never read her comic strip, he was going to suspect something eventually. The very fact that she hadn't grabbed the ring from his hand and slid it onto her finger should have told him that she had doubts about their union.

Traci sighed. Daniel was a catch by any definition. So what was her problem? She kept waiting to be struck by that sunny ray of happiness. Daniel said he wanted to take care of her, to fulfill her every wish. And he was even willing to let her think about it before she gave him her answer.

Guilt nibbled at her. She should be dancing up and down, not wavering like a weather vane in a gale.

Pronouncing the strip completed, she scribbled her signature in the corner of the last frame and then sighed. Another week's work put to bed. She glanced at the pile of mail on the counter. She'd been bringing it in steadily from the mailbox since Monday, but the stack had gotten no farther than her kitchen. Sorting letters seemed the least heinous of all the annoying chores that faced her.

Traci paused as she noted a long envelope. Morgan Brigham. Why would Morgan be writing to her?

Curious, she tore open the envelope and quickly scanned the short note inside.

Dear Traci,

I'm putting the summerhouse up for sale. Thought you might want to come up and see it one more time before it goes up on the block. Or make a bid for it yourself. If memory serves, you once said you wanted to buy it. Either way, let me know. My number's on the card.

Take care,
Morgan

P.S. Got a kick out of *Traci on the Spot* this week.

Traci folded the letter. He read her strip. She hadn't known that. A feeling of pride silently coaxed a smile to her lips. After a beat, though, the rest of his note seeped into her consciousness. He was selling the house.

The summerhouse. A faded white building with brick trim. Suddenly, memories flooded her mind. Long, lazy afternoons that felt as if they would never end.

Morgan.

She looked at the far wall in the family room. There was a large framed photograph of her and Morgan standing before the summerhouse. Traci and Morgan. Morgan and Traci. Back then, it seemed their lives had been permanently intertwined. A bittersweet feeling of loss passed over her.

Traci quickly pulled the telephone over to her on the counter and tapped out the number on the keypad.

* * * * *

Look for TRACI ON THE SPOT
by Marie Ferrarella, coming to
Silhouette YOURS TRULY
in March 1997.

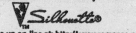

Silhouette

SPECIAL EDITION ™

WELCOME TO SILVER CREEK COUNTY

A place full of small-town Texas charm, where everybody knows your name and falling in love is all in a day's work!

Award-winning author **SHARON DE VITA** has spun several delightful stories full of matchmaking kids, lonely lawmen, single parents and humorous townsfolk! Watch for the first two books,
THE LONE RANGER
(Special Edition #1078, 1/97)
and
THE LADY AND THE SHERIFF
(Special Edition #1103, 5/97).
And there are many more heartwarming tales to come!

So come on down to Silver Creek and make a few friends—you'll be glad you did!

COMING NEXT MONTH

#1087 ASHLEY'S REBEL—Sherryl Woods
The Bridal Path
That Special Woman!
Forbidden passions sparked to life when ex-model Ashley Wilde
reluctantly shared very close quarters with handsome rebel Dillon Ford.
Can their turbulent past together allow them a passionate tomorrow?

#1088 WAITING FOR NICK—Nora Roberts
Those Wild Ukrainians
Here is the story readers have been begging for! To Frederica Kimball,
it seemed she'd spent her entire childhood waiting for Nick. Now she's
all grown up—and the waiting is over!

#1089 THE WRONG MAN...THE RIGHT TIME—Carole Halston
It was love at first sight when virginal Pat Tyler encountered ruggedly
handsome Clint Adams. But the ex-marine gallantly pushed the
beguiling young woman away. He thought he was the wrong man for
her. Could she convince him he was Mr. Right?

#1090 A HERO'S CHILD—Diana Whitney
Parenthood
Hank Flynn died a hero—or so everyone thought. Now he was back to
claim his fiancée—and the daughter he never knew he had....

#1091 MARRY ME IN AMARILLO—Celeste Hamilton
Gray Nolan would do anything to stop his baby sister's wedding—
even seduce bridal consultant Kathryn Seeger to his side. But this
commitment-shy cowboy quickly learned that Kathryn had no intention
of changing his sister's mind about marriage, and every intention of
changing his....

#1092 SEPARATED SISTERS—Kaitlyn Gorton
Single mom Ariadne Palmer just discovered she has a missing twin
sister! Placing her trust in the mysterious man who brought her this
compelling news, she must learn what family *really* means....

As seen on TV!
Free Gift Offer

With a Free Gift proof-of-purchase from any Silhouette® book, you can receive a beautiful cubic zirconia pendant.

This gorgeous marquise-shaped stone is a genuine cubic zirconia—accented by an 18" gold tone necklace.

(Approximate retail value $19.95)

Send for yours today...
compliments of ▼ *Silhouette*®
TM

To receive your free gift, a cubic zirconia pendant, send us one original proof-of-purchase, photocopies not accepted, from the back of any Silhouette Romance™, Silhouette Desire®, Silhouette Special Edition®, Silhouette Intimate Moments® or Silhouette Yours Truly™ title available in February, March and April at your favorite retail outlet, together with the Free Gift Certificate, plus a check or money order for $1.65 U.S./$2.15 CAN. (do not send cash) to cover postage and handling, payable to Silhouette Free Gift Offer. We will send you the specified gift. Allow 6 to 8 weeks for delivery. Offer good until April 30, 1997 or while quantities last. Offer valid in the U.S. and Canada only.

Free Gift Certificate

Name: _____

Address: _____

City: _____ State/Province: _____ Zip/Postal Code: _____

Mail this certificate, one proof-of-purchase and a check or money order for postage and handling to: SILHOUETTE FREE GIFT OFFER 1997. In the U.S.: 3010 Walden Avenue, P.O. Box 9077, Buffalo NY 14269-9077. In Canada: P.O. Box 613, Fort Erie, Ontario L2Z 5X3.

FREE GIFT OFFER   084-KFD
ONE PROOF-OF-PURCHASE
To collect your fabulous FREE GIFT, a cubic zirconia pendant, you must include this original proof-of-purchase for each gift with the properly completed Free Gift Certificate.

084-KFD

You're About to Become a
Become a
Privileged
Woman

Reap the rewards of fabulous free gifts and benefits with proofs-of-purchase from Silhouette and Harlequin books

Pages & Privileges™

It's our way of thanking you for buying our books at your favorite retail stores.

PROOF OF PURCHASE
SSE-PP22
Offer expires March 31,1997

Harlequin and Silhouette— the most privileged readers in the world!

For more information about Harlequin and Silhouette's PAGES & PRIVILEGES program call the Pages & Privileges Benefits Desk: 1-503-794-2499

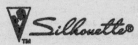

Silhouette®

SSE-PP22